CLOSE QUARTERS

BOOKS BY MARISSA PIESMAN

HEADING UPTOWN

PERSONAL EFFECTS

UNORTHODOX PRACTICES

THE YUPPIE HANDBOOK (with Marilee Hartley)

CLOSE QUARTERS

A NINA FISCHMAN MYSTERY

MARISSA PIESMAN

Delacorte Press

Published by
Delacorte Press
Bantam Doubleday Dell Publishing Group, Inc.
1540 Broadway
New York, New York 10036

ISBN 0-385-30538-9

Manufactured in the United States of America

AUTHOR'S NOTE

I would like to extend thanks to Robin Binder and Judy Kaufman, both seasoned Fire Island vets, for being so helpful. Thanks also go to my editor, Jackie Farber, her assistant, Diana Scarbrough, my publicist, Judy Westerman, and everyone else at Delacorte Press who made writing this book such a pleasure. And, as always, I couldn't have done it without the support of my agent, Janet Manus, and my husband, Jeffrey Marks.

CHAPTER 1

It wasn't until they were lined up for the Davis Park ferry that Nina remembered how much she hated the sun. When Cheryl had suggested a week at Fire Island, Nina thought about a lot of things, mostly having to do with shorts and bathing suits and other hopeless items of clothing. What she hadn't thought about was that she was basically a cold-weather mammal who had to walk around in long djellabas, lifting her hair up to schmear number fifteen sunblock on the back of her neck every half hour. And here she was in the blazing heat, surrounded by people who had been born with more than their share of melanin.

Cheryl, for example. It wasn't something Nina had thought about in the office, where Cheryl Schneiderman had just seemed like another white-girl lawyer under her suits and long-sleeved blouses. Now that the Ann Taylor ensembles had been shed, there emerged a dusky, sylphlike creature with a heliotropic tendency to turn her face into the sun whenever the opportunity arose.

Besides, all these dark creatures seemed to know one another. They squeezed each other's elbows and called each other babe and dug into their coolers and passed around cans of beer. Cheryl was doing a fair amount of elbow squeezing herself, periodically introducing Nina to someone who would ask her how it was going. It was going fine, except that she was already feeling the beginning effects of sunburn and prickly heat and she hadn't even made it onto the boat yet.

Nina fumbled around in her bag for an elastic band, found one and put up her hair. She usually tried to avoid ponytails for fear of appearing microcephalic. Voluminous tresses were more flattering. But it was so damn hot, she'd risk looking like a pinhead in order to catch a breeze on her sweaty shoulders.

"Jesus, it's hot," Cheryl said. "Want this?" She handed Nina the rest of a can of Bud Light that a man named J.J. in a Led Zeppelin T-shirt had given her.

"Okay. Thanks." Nina held the beer against her neck for a moment and then took a long hit.

"You'll feel cooler once we get on the boat."

"I feel cooler already. Can I finish this?"

"Sure," Cheryl said. "You're getting into the spirit of things pretty quickly."

"Why? Does a lot of boozing go on out there?"

"You might say that. It depends on what you compare it to."

"Compared to Fair Harbor?"

Cheryl smiled. "Oh, yeah. Compared to Fair Harbor, Davis Park is a regular gin mill."

Fair Harbor was all that Nina knew of Fire Island. She had taken a share out there a couple of summers ago. A half-share, actually, coming out on alternate weekends. She had a good enough time, but there had been too many protracted discussions about who ate whose yogurt and long debates about whether to buy skim or two percent milk. Nina had decided not to return. Cheryl had also spent a summer at Fair Harbor, but had switched to Davis Park eight years ago and had never gone back.

"But it's not fair to compare this place to Fair Harbor. That town isn't normal," Cheryl said.

"What do you mean?"

"All those shrinks and all those married couples with their kids. Who could have a good time?"

It was true, Fair Harbor had an inordinate number of therapists. Also legal aid lawyers. And many of the legal aid lawyers had married many of the therapists and now had children with Old Testament names. "Every time I went for a walk on the beach," Cheryl continued, "I had to listen to some damn social worker saying to her six-year-old brat, 'Now, Benjamin, does that make you angry? Why don't you use your words to express your anger?' It made me sick."

Nina knew what she meant. She hated people like that. She also wanted to be one. "I guess," she said.

"And those people don't drink. The only alcohol we kept in my house in Fair Harbor was white wine. And we only went through about a bottle a weekend."

Many Jewish women, despite all the cultural advances made in the last generation, remained almost uniformly steadfast teetotalers. When they saw alcohol, they thought calories. The fun factor seemed to elude them. Maybe it was biochemical. "I know," Nina said. "They all drink wine spritzers out there, heavy on the seltzer. The Jewish girl's drink of choice."

"I don't know if Jewish has anything to do with it," Cheryl said. "Look at us. I would never fuck up my wine by putting seltzer in it. And you seem like you can hold your own."

Nina didn't drink often, but when she did drink, it was with a seriousness of purpose. Impotent wine spritzers were not on her menu. And then she could forget about it for weeks, even months. The way she used to bum half a dozen Marlboros off someone, especially while drinking, and then never touch another cigarette for a year.

That was why it made her think it was all biochemical, that the psychological construct of the addictive personality had its limitations. Because she certainly couldn't do the same with food. Or fiction. Once she was in the middle of a good book, she'd stay up all night, avoid people, not answer the phone, even go in late to work in order to keep reading. Food, fiction . . . and then there was men. Another problem area.

Which was what had gotten her here to begin with. She'd held off making vacation plans until the last minute. Not that she assumed Tom would spend his vacation with her. Assumptions weren't her style. But when he told her that he was taking Annie, his six-year-old daughter, on a two-week canoe trip in July, she realized that she had been counting on him.

After all, weren't vacations the most important part of a long-distance relationship? Weekends were so short. By the time one of them had traversed the three hundred miles that separated Tom and Nina, it was almost time to turn around again.

Nina took Tom's news as a harbinger of doom, an indication that the relationship Wasn't Going Anywhere. Of course, on a rational level, she understood. He only got to see Annie once a week. And she was a charming child. Probably a better canoer than Nina too. But he had handed her the news so straightforwardly. Without apology. Not followed by "but we'll go to Paris in the fall" or anything.

It was the beginning of the end and Nina was disappointed. Also a little bit pissed. Which was probably why Nina had taken Cheryl seriously when she mentioned Fire Island. Not that Nina never took her seriously. Cheryl was great in court, a regular spitfire, hammering home her points over and over until everybody else just gave up. But the same tenacity carried over to the rest of her life. And coupled with a strong sense of justice, it made Cheryl a pain in the ass.

Every day, she'd march into Nina's office, sputtering and fuming about something or other. If it wasn't an unbelievably unfair judicial ruling, it was some man who didn't call or some dry cleaner that had cracked a button. She was the queen of Let's Make a Big Deal, which was probably what you needed to be in order to successfully litigate, Nina suspected.

But she couldn't figure out how Cheryl survived. It took so much energy to sputter and fume, to right every wrong. Cheryl's self-righteousness was like having an immunological disease. Nina, on the other hand, tried hard to immunize herself against all disappointments.

Hate being a lawyer? Be glad that you're not working in a nineteenth-century textile mill. Boyfriend disappears when it comes time to make vacation plans? Well, at least he didn't steal your electronic equipment. Nina tried to think of it as a highly developed coping mechanism, but sometimes she felt as if she were stuffing herself into an emotional cocoon. Her mantra had become *nicht gefairlach,* Yiddish for "it's not so terrible."

Although she had to admit that Tom had made her angry. Which was what had drawn her to Cheryl for advice. Nina wanted to fuel her sense of injustice and Cheryl was the perfect person to do so. "He had no right to do that," Cheryl had said. "He actively misled you. You don't go out with someone for over a year, making her schlep upstate in the middle of blizzards and thunderstorms for a crummy forty-eight hours together, and then drop her when there's an opportunity to spend some quality time together."

It made Nina feel better. "The hell with him," Cheryl had gone on. "Do something else. Come out to Fire Island with me. I'm going out on the Friday of July Fourth weekend. And I'm staying the whole week. My roommate wants to sell her share. Why don't you use the ten days as a free trial run. If you like it, you can buy into the rest of the summer. If not, forget about it, nothing lost."

"Why does she want to sell her share?" Nina had asked cautiously. Did Cheryl perform voodoo rites in her bedroom at night? Was the house filled with yogurt snatchers? Or worse yet, people who watched over their yogurt like temple guard dogs? Was this a trap that Nina was walking into?

"She sort of had a falling out with someone in the house. And now she's trying to avoid him."

"You mean she slept with him?"

"Right. A common mistake that people make out there."

"Sleeping with your housemate?"

"Sleeping with your housemate in June. You should at least wait until mid-August, when it can only ruin a small fraction of your summer."

"I'll keep that in mind," Nina had said.

"Does that mean you're interested?"

"What the hell. It beats enduring ten days in Westhampton Beach watching my sister spend her afternoons deciding which tablecloth to use for dinner."

So Nina had run out and bought a new bathing suit, an experience she only put herself through once every three years. Like getting her apartment painted. She also bought a bunch of garments that looked like boxer shorts but managed to cover most of the offending area. And now here she was, in a pair of men's underwear, boarding the Davis Park ferry. And already looking for shade.

CHAPTER 2

Anywhere a ferry pulls into looks good. It doesn't have to be Sausalito; it can be Staten Island and it will still have an air of romance about it. Davis Park looked particularly good to Nina.

The dock area was filled with tan people in loose white garments, waving with one hand and dragging little red wagons with the other. The scene had a feeling of fantasy about it, like the time Nina had arrived at Club Med and been greeted by a band of camp counselorish G.O.'s, superb physical specimens doing ridiculous hand signals that signified "welcome."

"What's with the wagons?" Nina asked.

"Every house has one. Since there are no cars, we use them to schlep around groceries and luggage. They're perfect for the wooden boardwalks."

"Nice touch. Sort of whimsical." More whimsical than

your traditional shopping cart, which suffered from old-lady connotations.

"Didn't you have them in Fair Harbor?"

"Yeah, I guess we did. I must have blocked the whole summer out. All those fights about yogurt."

"Look, there's Barry." Cheryl waved energetically to a tall man wearing mirrored sunglasses and holding a beer. He waved back lazily, letting his oversize white sleeve flap in the breeze.

"Is he in our house?"

"He *is* our house."

"What do you mean?" Nina felt like she was stuck in some toddler phase, asking "What's that?" and "What do you mean?" over and over.

"Didn't I tell you about Barry?"

"No, I don't think so."

"Oh." Cheryl paused. "Well, he's the house organizer. The one that gets the house together, and signs the lease and hooks up the phone and orders the groceries and all. In exchange, he gets to stay in the house for free. He has a single, the rest of us are doubled."

"How many of us would that be?"

"The house has six bedrooms. So that makes eleven, including you. But at least we all have full shares. The half-share houses are tough. You have to keep track of twice as many people. Weekends are the most crowded, of course. During the week, sometimes Barry has the house to himself."

"Oh, is he out here all week?"

"Yeah. He teaches school. Barry Adelman lives for the summer. He's a Davis Park institution."

Nina would never have pegged him as a schoolteacher. He looked sort of decayed, she thought. Maybe it was just the sunglasses. They gave him a hooded look, vaguely serpentine. Well, things were changing. Her mother's days of teaching school, with space shoes and support hose, were long gone. These days you probably *had* to cultivate the look of a drug dealer in order to relate to your students.

"He's been coming out here for ages. Probably almost twenty years," Cheryl said. "And he's always looking for new blood. Female blood. So steer clear."

"I don't think he's my type. I've always preferred the mammalian to the reptilian."

Cheryl laughed. "Yeah, Barry's not exactly cuddly. But he does have a certain kind of charm that can get under your skin. Believe me, I know. I learned the hard way."

The ferry nudged up against the dock and everyone lined up to disembark. "You had an affair with him?" Nina asked as she slung her bag over her shoulder.

"Last summer. A big mistake."

"And yet you went back into his house this summer?"

"You just don't understand how things work out here yet, Nina. Give yourself a couple of days. You'll see." As they climbed off the boat, Cheryl ran right over to Barry Adelman and gave him a huge hug.

"How ya doin'?" Barry placed his beerless hand on Cheryl's shoulder, while she kept her arms around his waist. They looked like the perfect eleventh-grade couple.

"Barry, this is Nina Fischman. She's staying out with me this week. She's sleeping in Mindy's bed."

"Oh, hi." Barry put his beer down in a nearby little red wagon and shook Nina's hand. "Nice to meet you."

"Same here."

"Ever been out before?"

"Not to Davis Park. But I had a share in a house in Fair Harbor one summer."

"Oh. Fair Harbor, huh?" He narrowed his eyes and critically appraised her. "Actually, I would have pegged you more as a Bayberry type."

"Bayberry? Never heard of it. Where is it?"

"Nowhere, anymore," Cheryl said. "The feds tore it down years ago. For the National Seashore. Almost everyone ended up moving their houses someplace else."

"How did they do that?"

"Mostly by barge. Barry, Nina's too young to have gone to Bayberry. You're losing all sense of time out here. Besides, she's not really the type. You don't wear Birkenstocks and flannel shirts, do you?"

Nina shook her head in the negative, since she knew it was a test of some sort. But of course, back in what were probably the Bayberry days she had a vast collection of plaid flannel shirts. Did being a Bayberry type mean wearing them back then, or still wearing them now? It probably didn't warrant a discussion.

"Well, I guess we'll find out if you're a Davis Park type this week, won't we?" Barry said. "C'mon, ladies, let's go get the groceries." He let go of Cheryl and pulled the wagon over to a nearby shed. She and Nina followed.

"The food comes over on the boat," Cheryl explained. "And we pick it up here and take it home in the wagon."

"There's no food on the island?"

"There's a store in town. Right over there." Cheryl pointed to a small grocery store next to an ice cream stand. "But it's really just for the *Times* and bagels. And for when we run out of milk."

The *Times*, bagels, and milk. And toilet paper and coffee. That was the extent of Nina's usual shopping list. Supplemented with take-out Chinese food, it made a full-enough life. She looked at the cartons of groceries that Barry was loading onto the wagon. The thought of being in proximity to boxes of Wheat Thins, wedges of Brie, and bags of nacho chips was suddenly unnerving. She pictured herself as the

Cosmic Cruncher, chomping her way through all five boxes, cardboard and all.

She looked closer. Two of the boxes contained liquor. House brands of vodka, gin, and rum, a couple of oversize bottles of white wine and plenty of beer, both light and regular. There were also cartons of pineapple juice, cans of something called Coco Lopez, and lots of tonic water. It was as if someone had ordered the fixings for a marathon cocktail party. Nina felt light-headed just examining the contents of the wagon.

Barry took their luggage, threw it on top of the groceries, and pulled the wagon inland, away from the dock, toward the house. Davis Park was more beautiful than Fair Harbor, with trees growing over the boardwalks, giving it the look of a tropical paradise. Sort of.

They made slow progress, since Barry had to stop and say hello to every third person that passed. "How ya doin'? How ya doin'?" He kept up a steady mumble accompanied by a constant forearm press. Cheryl seemed to know a fair number of the passersby also, and generously introduced Nina to the more acceptable-looking half of her acquaintances.

They seemed a diverse lot. Nina mentally tried to categorize them, a technique she had found comforting since childhood. Her shrink friend had told her it was a symptom of a hysterical personality. She didn't think of herself as hysterical; it was too upper middle class. But maybe that's what she was—a good old-fashioned hysteric.

As each person passed by, she scanned them like a state-of-the-art supermarket checkout device. But no apparent pattern emerged. Age, ethnicity, socioeconomic level, they were all over the map. The only generalization she could comfortably make was that everyone was pretty tan. Nina felt like a snow leopard that had forgotten to grow back her spots once spring came.

Except for one guy, a blond with very pink skin. He looked out of place, not only because of his complexion, but because of his shirt. It was an ordinary white cotton shirt, slightly baggy, button-down, probably oxford. The kind of shirt you see a thousand times a day in the city. But out here, among the tees and tanks, its tails flopping out over khaki shorts, it looked strange. Like an artifact from another culture. Wearing such a shirt made a statement of some sort. Nina just couldn't figure out what it was this guy meant to say. But he seemed affable enough when introduced and Nina soon forgot about him and resumed her computer scan of the rest of the passing parade.

Most of the people Barry greeted were women, and even though he barely varied his "How ya doin'?" they gave him a wide range of responses. Some squealed his name excitedly, squeezing his arm right back, inquiring as to his whereabouts for the rest of the weekend. He remained steadily evasive, alternating between "Who knows?" and "We'll see." Many of the other women seemed distinctly less enthusiastic, just giving him a small nod and a quick "Barry" and not breaking stride.

Nina took another look at him. He was attractive, even though not her type, as she had told Cheryl. He was tall and thin and tightly muscled, with a nicely protruding shelf to his behind.

Because of the mirrored sunglasses, she couldn't catch a glimpse of the windows of his soul, but the lower half of his face had a loose-lipped look that she had always equated with a lack of intelligence. It reminded her of the teenagers who used to hang out in front of the candy store when she was a little kid, the boys combing their greasy hair and the girls holding transistor radios up to their rollered heads. Yeah, that was it. Barry Adelman was an updated hood.

Nina knew she wasn't in dangerous territory here. Barry

had no interest in her; there would be no need to work hard to resist his serpentine charms. He had as much as told her so. She was a Bayberry type, not a Barry type. She swelled with pride. Suddenly Bayberry, wherever it had been, seemed like a glorious lost empire, the cradle of civilization. She regretted that her suitcase contained not one flannel shirt.

"Here we are, Nina. There's the house." Cheryl pointed ahead. "What do you think?"

Approaching from the side, both the front and rear decks were visible. The front deck looked almost directly out over the bay. "It looks great."

They turned off the boardwalk and climbed a few stairs to the front deck. Barry dropped the handle of the wagon and fell into a chair to finish his beer. "Come in, I'll give you a tour," Cheryl said.

"Okay." Nina followed her into the house. It contained a nice sweep of common space, the living, dining, and cooking areas all spilling into each other. "It's terrific, but where do we sleep?" Nina tried to picture eleven people spending the night. Twelve, if you counted one of those women whose elbows Barry was squeezing.

"The bedrooms are down underneath. Except for Barry's."

So not only did he get a single, but he also rated the only nonsubterranean bedroom. What was this, some kind of Charles Manson arrangement? Because Nina had no intention of playing Squeaky Fromme to any superannuated juvenile delinquent.

"C'mon," Cheryl said. "I'll make us a drink while we put away the groceries."

"Okay." Nina shrugged. "I guess."

CHAPTER 3

As soon as the last grocery item was put away, Cheryl mixed up a blenderful of piña coladas. The kitchen was a haphazard collection of throwaway pots and pans, dented and thin-bottomed, chipped Fiesta ware, and tinny forks with a one-out-of-four bent-tine ratio. But the blender was a beauty, sleek and polished, prominently displayed in the center of what was once a handsome butcher-block counter.

Cheryl mixed like an expert, not bothering to measure the rum, ice, pineapple juice, or Coco Lopez. Barry followed the sounds of the whirring blender from the deck into the kitchen. He pulled his sunglasses off and hooked them onto his shirt. Nina was taken by her first glimpse of his eyes. They were an unusual shade for a human being, not quite the pure yellow of a cat's eyes, but too yellow to be called green. There was a ring around the iris, and the dark part bled into the yellow in a strange pattern. As if he had crystal formations in his eyes.

Barry gave Cheryl one of his famous Adelman elbow squeezes and stuck his nose into the pitcher of drinks. Nina was so fascinated by his eyes that she found herself stooping over to stare at them through the glass. Which didn't work, since the sides of the blender were opaque with colada. At least now Nina knew what those cans of Coco Lopez were for. This new piece of information made her feel cool, like a seasoned Fire Island vet.

"Get your nose out of there," Cheryl said, giving Barry a poke in the ribs. There was a lot of physical contact out here. Nina would have to get used to it. In the city, you could go months without anyone touching you, except for occasionally getting your foot stepped on in the subway.

"Cheryl makes the best piñas," Barry said. "And you know what makes them the best?"

"What's that?"

"The fact that she makes them so often. It's always piña time around here."

"That's true." Cheryl added a handful of ice cubes and gave the blender another whir. "Last summer we went through two blenders. So this year we invested in a heavy-duty, industrial-strength Waring. So far it's been holding up pretty well."

"It did stand out," Nina said, "against the rest of the kitchen debris."

"We're not a foodie house, if that's what you're looking for," Barry said, sounding a tiny bit nasty. "If you want great meals, you're in the wrong place. But there are houses in Davis Park that are into that sort of thing."

"Yeah," said Cheryl, "like over at Kevin's. It's a regular four-star restaurant there. He's the master chef and the rest of the house get to be his assistants. They spend every weekend in the kitchen, following orders. They never get to the beach—they're too busy marinating."

"Kevin's a real kitchen Nazi," Barry said. "But he does turn out some fine cuisine. Remember the full-moon party they had last month? There were the best hors d'oeuvres."

"There were." Cheryl poured out a round of drinks. "They really broke their backs on that one. Little beggars' purses stuffed with sour cream and red caviar and tied with a scallion strand. Very labor-intensive."

"And goat cheese in everything. On minipizzas, baked into mushrooms, stuffed into pea pods. We started calling the house Chez Chèvre after that." Barry paused to sample his drink. He gave Cheryl a wink to show his approval. Then he turned to Nina. "So if you're into goat cheese, that's the house for you. But if you're more interested in a really fine piña colada every hour on the hour, you've come to the right place."

Nina took a long hit from her glass to show that she was no teetotaling foodie wimp. "Cheryl, this might be the best piña colada I've ever tasted. What's your secret?"

"A practiced eye." Cheryl managed to get half of hers down at once. "God, I'm so glad to be here." She walked over and threw herself onto the couch. All of the furniture had been covered with white sheets, tied down with twine around the legs. It gave the place an airy, casual look. A clever way to look chic for under twenty-five dollars. Maybe these people were onto something. Nina wondered how it would look in her living room. Probably like the place was inhabited by a demented shopping-bag lady with a bed-linen fetish.

She was just about to sit down in one of the sheet-covered chairs when Cheryl suddenly jumped up. "We're missing too much sun," she said.

"You're an addict. At least let Nina finish her drink before you drag her off to the beach." Barry looked at Nina in a way that he hadn't before. This time she got a good, long look at his eyes. The little crystal formations were lacy and intricate, and she had to work hard to suppress her desire to visually trace each and every one of them. Despite herself.

Cheryl picked up her glass and the half-empty blender. "Well, let's at least go out on the deck."

"Okay, okay." Barry took Nina by the arm. "Let me put some sunblock on," he told her. "We are a modern household. We take precautions." He increased his pressure on her arm ever so slightly, to punch up the double entendre.

Nina felt that fluttery ooze coming on. It had been a while. The man was a master, despite the fact that they so clearly weren't each other's type, that he reminded her of a dumb hood and she reminded him of flannel shirts and Bayberry. But he was an alchemist, capable of spontaneous combustion, of creating a chemical reaction without any chemicals. She couldn't fight it; he was too good.

Was she in for trouble this summer? Probably not. Barry wasn't serious. He had casually gotten her going, without really trying. Surely if she pushed it, showed up in his bed naked or something, he'd cooperate. But she had a feeling she wasn't on his hit list, that arm squeezes and double entendres were like breathing and peeing to him, acts performed primarily by involuntary muscles. And as long as she stayed out of range, she'd be all right. He wasn't going to go out of his way, departing from his normal trajectory, to hit on her.

Unless he had run out of women. But judging by the walk back from the ferry, he still had quite a female following. As far as she could tell, he had received a pretty enthusiastic response to most of his elbow squeezing. However, Cheryl had said he was always looking for new blood. Maybe all those elbows were last summer's body parts. Like Cheryl herself. After all, she had said that her affair with Barry had ended badly, and she was still squeezing back. It was confusing. Nina wasn't familiar with the customs of the local gentry.

"Believe me," she said, to hammer the point home, "I

take precautions. I know how to protect myself. I'm not the type to get burned."

"I see you brought us a tough broad, Cheryl. Is she one of your mouthpiece friends?"

It took Nina a few seconds to figure out that mouthpiece meant lawyer, one of those words from old gangster movies. When she remembered, she was relieved. She wouldn't have to subject everyone to a lecture about the First Amendment, about a woman's right to have a big mouth. It was easier to join in casting aspersions on a profession universally considered odious.

"Yeah, I'm a lawyer," she said, tough but kidding. "You got a problem with that?"

"No, not at all. It's good to know a lot of lawyers. You never know when you might be in need of their services." As he spoke, he put his sunglasses back on. The crystal formations disappeared and he looked like a dumb hood again. Nina wondered exactly what kind of legal services he might be in need of. "Shall we, ladies?" He held the door open for them. They went out and arranged themselves on various pieces of deck furniture.

"What do *you* do?" Nina had never found an interesting, graceful way to phrase the question. "What's your line?" she would sometimes try, in a snappy, fifties voice, but it always fell flat. Of course, she knew the answer to the question. Cheryl had told her what Barry did. But that didn't matter. Once asked, you had to ask back.

Obligatory in New York, anyway. She had spent a month in South America, practicing her high school Spanish, years ago. No one had asked her what she did for a living. Not once, in a whole month. It would have been relaxing, except that she was relentlessly barraged by inquiries as to how many children she had.

"I teach school," Barry said. "Junior high."

"What subject?"

"Hard to say. Behavior, mostly. They give me the kids that no one else can do anything with. And I try to get them to sit still for two periods at a time. Then I let them loose on someone else."

"That's it?"

"I also try to teach them to read a little bit."

"I see. Where does this take place?"

"Bushwick."

To Nina, Bushwick was about as alien as a territory could get. It was in the deep recesses of Brooklyn, a place where even the IRT didn't go. If someone handed her a map of New York City, she wasn't so sure she could even find Bushwick. Had Joseph Conrad written a novel about Brooklyn instead of Africa, Bushwick would be his heart of darkness.

"How do you get there?" Despite her years as a sophisticated Manhattanite, she was still at heart a Bronx girl who had a hard time believing that anybody really took the BMT to work every day.

"Car pool. In an armored car."

"I can imagine. And where do you eat lunch?"

It sounded irrelevant, but Nina had her reasons for asking. She had often wondered what she would have done if she hadn't gone to law school. She usually pictured herself teaching in an inner-city school somewhere. The way some people had phobias about being killed in a plane crash, Nina had an irrational fear of suddenly being transformed into a ghetto teacher, probably on the junior high level. And she always wondered where she would eat lunch. "You don't have to bring your lunch, do you?" She couldn't picture Barry Adelman packing himself a sandwich every morning. He wasn't exactly the wholesome, lunchbox type. Maybe he even skipped lunch and drank black coffee and Jack Daniel's.

"There's a pizza parlor around the corner. Also a *cuchifrito* place down the block. And a shish kebab guy with a cart."

That was reassuring, in case her fears ever came true. Because Nina had a thing about bringing her lunch. Brown bagging had unliberated connotations for her, a continuation of years of domestic slavery. Somehow, if the only thing that came out of decades of feminist struggle was the freedom to eat lunch out . . . well, it wasn't quite *Roe* v. *Wade*, but it was something. The real pinnacle of equality was ordering a beverage with your lunch. Most women hadn't evolved to that stage yet.

It was typical of her, Nina thought, to ask him something like where he ate lunch. While there he was, day in and day out, struggling to save young minds and souls from falling into permanent despair. His work had to be somewhat interesting, no matter how jaded he was. The way hers was. As a staff attorney with Legal Services for the Elderly, a federally funded project, she always had at least a few good stories to tell. But when someone presented her with that cosmic request—tell me about your work—some sort of ennui would take over. Instead of letting a true sense of commitment rise to the surface, all of her discontents and doubts would seize hold of her. And usually all she could manage was a discussion about where she ate lunch, in a small voice.

"How long have you been teaching there?" It was a step up from lunch, but not quite hitting high philosophical heights.

"All my life. Feels like. Actually, I taught in the Bronx for eleven years and I've been in Brooklyn for about as long. So it looks like I'm up for retirement pretty soon. I can retire with a decent pension after twenty-five."

"And then what?"

"Who knows? Teaching's all I've ever done. I started

when they took away my grad school deferment and never left."

"He's hooked on Fire Island," Cheryl said. "At this point, Barry couldn't bear a job that didn't give him his summers off."

"I do like it out here." He held his glass out to Cheryl for a refill.

"When Labor Day comes around, he practically has to be medicated."

Nina could imagine. On a teacher's salary, he probably had some small, crummy apartment somewhere. And not enough discretionary income to entertain himself properly. Out here in Davis Park, he had the run of the place. There was nothing really to spend money on. Everyone dressed casually, and you couldn't tell a schoolteacher from a banker. A decent haircut and an expensive pair of sunglasses were all you needed, just a few props. And Barry had those eyes. Which in the city couldn't get him into pricey restaurants or health clubs, but on Fire Island could probably gain him entry into any situation he desired.

"What's on the agenda for this weekend, Barry?" Cheryl asked. "Who's coming out?"

"Everyone. The house is going to be packed. Hope you don't tend toward the claustrophobic, Nina."

She never used to. She had been born in a boom year, and everything she had attended was packed. Her elementary school classes had enrollments exceeding forty. Kids sat on the windowsills. Her junior high school was on split session. And despite the special funding that the Bronx High School of Science had received in the postsputnik years, they were still four to a microscope. The Y camps she went to stuffed double the usual number into each cabin, using bunk beds. And in her college dorm, she had been tripled most of the time. Her law school had been opened especially to catch the big surge of baby boom enrollment, and as a result had no ivy or stone. Just brand-new blackboard erasers. And young law professors that were afraid to use the Socratic method on a student body that wore overalls and hissed whenever a teacher used the gender-specific pronoun "he."

And when she had returned to New York to practice law, she had squeezed into an Upper West Side rental with three other women, then finally wedged herself into her own tiny one-bedroom. So tiny that when she neglected to hang up her terry cloth bathrobe, Nina felt as though another person had moved in.

So by now she should have developed a generational immunity to claustrophobia. But she had lost it somewhere along the road. And the thought of eleven people sitting in the living room made her panicky. She checked the sky, fearing rain. So far it looked clear, but you never knew what might blow in tomorrow.

"Could I take a look at our bedroom?" Nina asked, trying to stay calm.

"Sure." Cheryl pointed to the right. "Down those stairs, last room on the right."

The downstairs had a tar paper feeling, as if it had been constructed as a stage set, meant to be torn down after a two-week run. The bedroom had the dimensions of a galley kitchen, with twin beds hardly wider than the average dishwasher. The bare striped mattress ticking was lumpy, like in a second-rate youth hostel. A small table separated the beds, on which there was a dime store ceramic lamp. Not even enough light to read by, thought Nina. She immediately felt struck by insomnia, even though it was only two o'clock in the afternoon.

CHAPTER 4

The sun seemed blinding when Nina emerged upstairs, out on the deck. But after the dingy, cheap motel feeling of the bedroom, sunlight was welcome. She was hit with a sudden, strong urge to get onto the beach. She supposed that was how the day went around here. You bounced between the claustrophobia of eleven people in a room to the agoraphobia of the Atlantic Ocean.

"I'd like to see the beach." Nina pulled her sunblock out of her purse.

"Suits me," said Cheryl. "Wanna come for a walk?"

"Not right now." Barry got up out of his deck chair and leaned into a runner's stretch. "I told Jenny I'd come over right about now."

"Jenny?" Cheryl asked sharply. "Does Angela know about this?"

"Who are you? The girlfriend monitor?"

"You're right. I'm sorry. Forget I said anything."

"I thought we had reached some sort of—"

"Okay, okay. I said you were right. I won't mention it again."

"Want some?" Nina offered her tube of number fifteen to Cheryl, mostly to break the tense silence.

"No, thanks. I'm already down to number two. By the end of the week, I'll definitely be ready for just baby oil."

Nina hadn't seen anyone use baby oil in decades. It was the drug of a hard-core addict, the equivalent of mainlining or freebasing. Baby oil let the sun right into your veins. "Hasn't baby oil been outlawed by now?"

"I know what I'm doing. I can handle it." More language of the addict. "I start out carefully, with number fifteen, cut with a little number four. By the end of the first weekend, I'm usually ready for number eight. Then I move downward gradually, only when appropriate."

"But it can't be good for you. I didn't think people still did this." Nina didn't think people still drank piña coladas every hour on the hour either. Or slept with both Jenny and Angela at the same time. Davis Park was like Brigadoon, a place where 1975 magically reappeared once a year.

"Who are you? The sunburn monitor?"

"Sorry."

Cheryl turned to Barry. "Did you sell my mother a share in this house without telling me?" She was making herself clear. Nina was on Cheryl's turf and she should kindly keep her mouth shut. They had quite a little pecking order here, a hierarchy with Nina on the bottom, Barry on top, and Cheryl in the middle.

"Ready to go to the beach?" Nina laced her ponytail through an old Yankee cap she had found in her closet. It had become popular to hate Steinbrenner. He had made it almost impossible to stick with the Yankees. But Nina just couldn't jump ship; she went so far back with them. She figured her Bronx childhood entitled her to an exemption from mandatory desertion.

"Let's go."

"Should we put our stuff in the bedroom?" Nina had an interior alarm that went off whenever she was more than ten yards from her handbag.

"Nah, we can leave it up here. There are things to worry about out here, but being ripped off isn't one of them."

The walk to the beach was glorious. The light-colored wooden boards were cool under their bare feet. And because there were no cars permitted on the island, the air had a quiet freshness that made Nina feel as though she were a thousand miles from New York.

Her first glimpse of the ocean didn't exactly change her life. She had seen it before. But after she and Cheryl had walked along the beach for a while, she started to feel different. The beach was pretty deserted, certainly less crowded than Fair Harbor and much emptier than the packed city beaches of her youth. And there was something about walking along a quiet beach, her feet in the cool water and her boxer shorts guarding against prickly heat, that gave Nina a feeling of privilege. She could have been a Kennedy in Hyannisport or a Bush in Kennebunkport. She could almost forget that she was an underpaid poverty attorney who owned one eleventh of a weekend.

Because being at the shore was like being in the ninety-ninth percentile. She knew that at any given moment, almost one hundred percent of the world's population was inland. So just standing with her feet in the water made Nina feel like she had a crown on her head.

"Where are we going?" she asked Cheryl.

"Going? This is Fire Island. There's no place to go." Nina was starting to feel a little bit like Alice. And Cheryl was developing an edge worthy of the Red Queen from *Through the*

Looking-Glass. "We're headed in the direction of Watch Hill. Although we're not going there," she said firmly. "And back that way," she added, pointing her thumb over her shoulder, "is Water Island. And we're not going there either. We're just going for a walk on the beach, that's all." The pecking order had been reestablished.

"Okay," Nina said, trying to sound as agreeable as possible. "I've been to Watch Hill. Tell me about Water Island."

"It's just a small community, very exclusive. No ferry service or anything. Everyone has their own boats. Perry Ellis used to have a house there."

The crown on Nina's head seemed to dissolve. Apparently you weren't really cool unless you had a house in a community with no ferry service. There was always something to make you feel like you hadn't quite arrived. "Is the beach always this empty?"

"Not always. Remember, it's the middle of a weekday afternoon. Although Fridays are always a little more crowded than earlier in the week. But the great thing about Davis Park, as opposed to Fair Harbor, is that it's the easternmost community. So you can keep walking in this direction forever. And once you get past the campground at Watch Hill, you'll never run into another soul."

"Kinda the end of the line, huh?"

"In more ways than one."

"What do you mean?" asked Nina.

"A lot of people start out in towns closer in, like Kismet." Nina had heard of the place. It was renowned for its gold chains. "When they get a little older, maybe they move on to Ocean Beach or Fair Harbor. If they get married and have kids, they might stay in Fair Harbor. Otherwise they drift eastward and end up here. No one ever gets too old for Davis Park."

Nina tried to picture herself at fifty, content with one

eleventh of a living space. She couldn't. When had this happened? When had the idealization of communal living faded? What happened to the idea of the commune, the kibbutz? When she was twenty, the thought of ending up in suburban isolation was deadly. Now she could think of worse things. It was sad that the notion of socialism, nurtured as a tiny spark by her grandparents in the shtetl, fanned to a hearty flame by her parents before the war, and tended by Nina herself up until a few years ago, should sputter and die so suddenly. For how could she pretend to still be a socialist when she wouldn't even pick up her phone without letting her answering machine screen her calls?

"There's the Casino." Cheryl interrupted Nina's historical/political internal monologue.

"The what?"

"The Casino. Colloquially known as the Caz. That, along with the ice cream stand, grocery store, and public telephone booths, constitute all of our major local attractions."

"Is it really a casino? Like in Atlantic City?"

"No gambling allowed. Except with your heart."

"What is it? Not a singles bar," Nina groaned.

"That and more. It's fast food during the day, happy hour at sunset, dinner at eight, and after that, anything you want. A place to dance or schmooze or drink yourself under the bar. It takes the place of a community center, pool hall, church supper, and public lavatory. Want to check it out?"

"Actually, I'm dying to go to the bathroom."

"Right this way." They climbed up a long wooden staircase from the beach and followed the walkway into the Casino. The place looked like the kind of bar that Nina usually tried to avoid. There were a couple of hard-core alkies attached to their stools and a bartender that looked like he had peaked in his junior year of high school.

It began to occur to Nina that she might not do too well

in a place like this. All her life, she had always harbored the notion that if she could only find the right *arena,* she'd have an easier time. The courtroom had proved a disappointment, as had singles' night at B'nai Jeshurun. The Casino probably wasn't going to be it either. She remained a woman without an arena.

Nina took a long, satisfying leak in the ladies' room. When she got out, Cheryl was leaning against the bar. "Wanna beer?" she asked Nina.

"I don't think so." It had felt so good to empty her bladder that she was reluctant to fill it up again.

"Okay, let's see what's going on at the house." Cheryl led her back through the maze of boardwalks in town. As they walked, Cheryl kept up a running commentary on the houses they passed. She seemed to know quite a bit about who lived where and who was sleeping with whom. She pointed to a particularly tidy-looking house with geraniums in the window boxes and a big deck overlooking the ocean. "That's Sunmist. They give the best parties. They had a black-and-white theme party a couple of weeks ago that was really wild."

"What do you mean?" To Nina, black and white meant those big cookies they sold in the bakeries of her childhood.

"You had to wear things that were black or white."

"Really?" Somehow Nina never saw herself in black and white. She never saw anything in black and white. She was a big fan of the gray area. "Why would you want to go to a party like that?"

"What do you mean, why? Because it's fun, that's why."

"Do people ever have to wear togas to parties?"

"This isn't *Animal House,* for Chrissakes. As a matter of fact, Sunmist is having a sunset party tonight. We'll go," Cheryl said very decisively.

"Do we have to wear anything special?"

"It's a jungle theme. You'll have to wear something jungly." Cheryl was starting to sound like the Red Queen again.

"I don't have anything jungly."

"We'll improvise."

"Does our house ever have parties?"

"No, because we're afraid the deck will fall down." They paused in front of another house, less tidy and without window boxes. "Let's stop in here for a minute."

"How come?"

"Because I want to." They walked in without knocking. "Anybody home?" Cheryl called. Nobody answered. "Oh, well, I guess he's at the beach."

"Who's at the beach?"

"Jonathan."

"Who's that?"

"You met him earlier this afternoon. On the way back from the ferry."

"I did? I don't remember. So what's the story? Are you maintaining an active interest in Jonathan?"

"Nope. Not my type," Cheryl said.

"How come?"

"Too mammalian. Not serpentine enough for me."

"That doesn't sound healthy." Maybe Cheryl should be going to theme therapy instead of theme parties. Of course, Nina didn't have the nerve to say so.

"We'll catch Jonathan later. Let's go back and see who arrived on the four o'clock ferry."

"How about giving me a preview?" Nina said. "Is there anything I should know about anybody beforehand?"

"Like what?"

"Who to hang around with, who to stay away from."

"No mass murderers this summer." Cheryl opened the door to leave. "As far as I know. Come on, let's go."

CHAPTER 5

Before the house even came into view, Nina heard the sounds of piña coladas being consumed by a large group of people. The group turned out to be composed exclusively of women, seven of them, and they were spread out on the deck.

Nina knew she should be disappointed. After all, this was to be more than just a vacation. Fire Island came under the category of a Place to Meet Men. And, like so many Places to Meet Men, the poetry readings, the hiking groups, even the Bar Association Subcommittee on Housing Issues, it seemed to be populated by women. Which should have turned Nina's mood foul, but it never did.

Quite the contrary. There she'd be, watching the door. And it would slowly become clear that whatever congregation she was a part of that day was yet another henhouse. And she'd get a warm feeling, a mix of recognition, intimacy, and relief. Her darting eye movements slowed down. Nina felt her eyebrows and chin lower to where they belonged, her spine lose its arch. She became herself again. And then she was usually off on a really good conversation with someone who either lived in her neighborhood or had gone to Bronx Science the year before Nina or knew someone who worked in her office.

She was aware that other women, upon arriving and surveying the gender mix in the room, were muttering "Oh, shit" under their breath and beating a hasty retreat. And she always felt some slight pressure to do the same. But talking to women who reminded Nina of herself was so much more fun than listening to men who had no idea who she was and considered it too much trouble to find out.

She felt the same guilt in spending all her time talking to women that she felt in eating between meals. The hasty retreaters were the strict dieters, the compulsive exercisers, the ones who kept themselves on a schedule and cut their losses. They wouldn't waste the time. But Nina always stayed on into the evening and had fun. It was like being back in the dorm, one of the best places in the world. She could spend her life this way.

Cheryl was probably a member of the school of hasty retreaters, because as soon as the deck came into view, she offered, by way of an apology, a quick "Don't worry. There *are* some men in the house. They're just not here yet."

"That's okay. I have no problem with the company of women." Nina tried to say it with pride, but she had that feeling again. The feeling that she was defending an indulgent act, like putting mayonnaise on her sandwich or skipping an aerobics class.

"The one in the red sweatshirt is from another house," Cheryl said, as if she were trying to better the odds. "Come on up, I'll introduce you."

One of the women was in the middle of a story, a loud

one, and she didn't stop for the arrival of Nina and Cheryl. "Can you believe it?" she said, winding up. "She had no idea the entire time. She thought he just had extremely thin eyebrows." The crowd broke up with laughter. When it had died down, Cheryl introduced Nina as Mindy's potential replacement.

"Poor Mindy," said a woman in a striped maillot. "Well, Nina, we hope you're not going to be Mindy's replacement in every sense of the word." The crowd broke up again, but more subdued this time.

"How about some discretion, Barbara?" Cheryl said.

"How about some piña coladas, Cheryl?" Barbara said.

Nina went into the kitchen and watched Cheryl make another batch. When they were settled on the deck with their drinks, Cheryl went around, giving names to the faces. Nina was an avid user of mnemonic devices, although her devices were quirky enough to render them useless to anyone else. There was a woman named Estelle, for example, whom she pictured as Stella, in Stanley Kowalski's arms. Another woman, named Harriet, had a fine black down over her forearms. For the rest of her stay, Nina would have to do a quick arm scan before she remembered—yes, that's hairy Harriet. Generally the method worked, although it wasn't foolproof. Nina never could remember Harriet's name when she was wearing long sleeves.

"Is everyone going to Sunmist tonight?" a woman named Debbie, who unfortunately bore no resemblance to Debbie Reynolds, asked. She was the one in the red sweatshirt, the one Cheryl had said was from another house. Nina didn't bother thinking up a mnemonic device for a mere neighbor, although she agonized over it for a moment or two.

"Of course we're all going. Who wouldn't?" asked a redhead named Nancy. Nancy was a tricky one. The best Nina could come up with was that redheads looked good in orange and that was *naranja* in Spanish, which shared its first two letters with Nancy. This stuff was exhausting. Why couldn't she be the kind of person who could look someone straight in the eye and say, "What's your name again?"

"They do give the best parties," said a woman named Maggie. She was an easy one. Maggie had a voice like a magpie. "Where's Ira?" she asked.

"He's coming," Estelle said. "He had to work a full day, so he's picking up Charlie at five and they're driving out."

"Are they crazy?" Maggie said. "You know what traffic on the LIE is going to be like? Friday afternoon before July Fourth weekend? They'll miss the last boat."

That was the good thing about Fire Island, compared to the Hamptons. You could take the train and arrive carless without being at a disadvantage. Since you had to leave your car over on the mainland, in Patchogue, everyone was trapped like rats, even if they owned a Lamborghini. It was very egalitarian.

"Where's Barry?" Nancy asked. She was the best-looking one, Nina decided, with her red hair and turquoise eyes. She hoped that Nancy wasn't wasting herself on that crystal-eyed vampire.

"Out in the alley, like any common tomcat," Cheryl said. She stood up suddenly. "I'm going to make some hors d'oeuvres."

"Need some help?" asked Harriet. She seemed to be the nice one, maybe to compensate for her hair.

"No," Cheryl said sharply. Too sharply. There was some sort of subplot here, but Nina could not yet tell what it was. Cheryl took off for the kitchen.

"Ever been to Davis Park before?" asked Elizabeth, a rather regal woman, with a high enough forehead to remind Nina of the Virgin Queen.

"No, but I had a share in Fair Harbor for one summer."

"Oh, Fair Harbor," Maggie squawked, and rolled her eyes.

"What's wrong with Fair Harbor?" asked Harriet, the nice one defending the nice community.

"Too many kids. Didn't you think so, Nina?"

"There were a lot of kids," she answered mildly. This was dangerous territory. Nina generally tried to think of herself as a nice type, like Harriet without the hair. A woman who liked children and small animals, who hadn't been left embittered by watching all her peers march off to the maternity ward. Always a visitor, never a patient. She could handle that. But there was no use denying that she was developing what she privately referred to as an OPC problem. Other People's Children.

They were charming and cute and cuddly and she wanted one desperately. But after ten minutes, an interior voice would pipe up, very haughty and all, and say, "Take them away." Maybe she was becoming defensive, or having a jealous reaction to Tom's six-year-old daughter.

Did this make her less nice? Probably. She was certainly less nice than the fourteen-year-old Nina Fischman who used to baby-sit for the four Greenberg children, ages 0–8, for seventy-five cents an hour. "She's so good with children," Mrs. Greenberg would tell everybody. "And so nice." "Take them away," Nina would say now, if stuck in a room for more than ten minutes with little Glenn, Stephanie, Scott, and Jamie Greenberg.

"I wasn't in a house with kids in Fair Harbor," Nina said.

"No, but the beach is littered with them." Maggie got a laugh out of everyone except Harriet. Nina found a small "ha" erupting from her own lips. When had she stopped being like Harriet and left behind the junior high school Nina? The Nina who had always been the designated nice one on the team, even though she didn't have hairy arms.

The truth was that it wasn't only children Nina had lost patience with. She was having trouble lately with a lot of adults too. Maybe this wasn't the right time to share a house with ten other people. And she used to suffer fools gladly. In fact, she used to suffer fools ecstatically. It had been one of her great talents.

She tried to relax and refocus on the conversation. Cheryl was back with cheese and crackers and more drinks, and the girls were discussing Barry Adelman, a topic that Nina guessed was a popular one in the house.

"Angela came by about half an hour ago, looking for him," Nancy said.

"Well, you know where he is, don't you?" asked Cheryl.

"I think I do, but I'm not sure. At Jenny's?"

"How did you guess?"

"It wasn't hard. When the boat pulled out last Sunday, I noticed that she had stayed behind. I figured it was only a matter of time."

"How old is she?" asked Nina.

"Jenny? Young. Why?"

"I figured she was. It's a young name. Unless she's British." She got blank stares from everyone except Barbara, the indiscreet one in the striped maillot.

"I know what you mean," Barbara said. "They didn't start naming people Jenny in the States until after we were born."

"Exactly." So it looked like Nina wasn't going to have to sit around all week suffering fools after all. "About the same time they started naming people Joshua."

"I think Jennifer came a little before Joshua," Barbara said. "They're both nice names. Too bad the masses have rendered them unusable."

"Actually, Jennifer's been abandoned from overuse. You could bring it back, I suppose."

"Maybe. But I have a feeling that the entire letter *J* has been usurped. You can't really name a kid anything beginning with a *J* and not sound trite."

Nina laughed. "Right. And now they're getting to the vowels. Allison, Emily, Eli, Evan, Ethan, even Isaac and Abraham are coming back. It makes you feel compelled to go with a consonant."

"There's always Ulysses and Uriah."

Nina had always felt that being childless should not prevent her from discussing baby names, one of life's great pleasures. And Barbara had a lot to say on the topic. Of course, it made Nina a little nervous to think that she could spend hours making up names for fictional children when she could no longer spend even minutes in the same room with real ones. But this thought got pushed to the rear of her cluttered mind.

"Don't forget Otis," Nina said. "It's one of my favorites."

Their reverie was interrupted by Cheryl. "What are you wearing to the party at Sunmist tonight?" she asked Nina.

"I don't know."

"Come with me. We're going to pick out an outfit for you."

She reluctantly followed Cheryl toward the bedroom, giving her new friend a mournful parting glance. "And Otto," she called to Barbara as she started down the stairs. "That's another good one, don't you think?"

CHAPTER 6

Nina kept tugging at her jumpsuit. The offending garment belonged to Cheryl, and it was just too short in the crotch. She was about Nina's height, but their torso-to-leg proportions were different. Nina always had the same problem with jumpsuits. She liked the idea of them: an unbroken line of color from neck to ankle was a good streamlining device. And they were incredibly comfortable, like her childhood Dr. Denton's. So hope sprung eternal, and she could never resist bringing a few into the dressing room, just to see.

Many times she thought she was going to get away with it, looking approvingly at her unbroken, streamlined self head-on in the dressing room mirror. But then she'd turn around and there it was again—the crotch creeping right up her crack. Her torso was just too damn long. And she'd have to hang the jumpsuit back up, because only early-nineteenth-century American presidents could get away with walking around with their crack showing. Besides, little Jamie Madison had a cuter tush.

But they had tried on everything in both Nina's and Cheryl's wardrobes, and Cheryl insisted that this jumpsuit gave Nina just the right jungly look. And that the crack was barely visible, mostly in Nina's imagination. And it was a tempting number, made from rayon in one of those new-but-made-to-look-old prints that made you feel like Bette Midler back in the Continental Baths days. So Nina had succumbed and here she was on the deck of Sunmist, tugging at her crotch and humming "Boogie Woogie Bugle Boy" under her breath.

The place was packed. Apparently both Angela *and* Jenny were there and the crowd was watching Barry to see what would happen. It had become increasingly clear over the course of the afternoon that Barry-watching was a favorite house sport. Now it seemed that the whole town indulged. And Barry was in fine form. He was wearing light green surgical scrubs. A stroke of genius, really. Jerry Seinfeld had come up with the observation that women respond to doctors the way that men respond to models. It was embarrassing but true. Every time Nina went to visit someone in the hospital, she found herself lusting after every doctor that crossed her path, even the homeliest, yarmulked, underage little resident. And here was Barry Adelman exuding the same aura, by virtue of donning two simple garments. The guy should be in marketing instead of wasting his days in Bushwick.

"I'm not a doctor in real life, but I play one at sunset parties," she said to Cheryl as Barry went by.

"Well, it seems to work." He had landed on a young, fresh-faced strawberry blonde with hair swinging down past her waist.

"Who's she?" Nina asked.

"Never saw her before. I told you, Barry maintains a taste for new blood."

"Well, I'd put my money on her waking up tomorrow with puncture marks."

"There's a good chance. Especially in light of what's going on in the corner." Cheryl pointed to two women engaged in serious conversation. "Jenny and Angela seem to have a few things to discuss. He's certainly not going to be spending the evening with either of them."

"Which one is which?"

"Jenny's on the left." She looked as young as the strawberry blonde, with similar coloring and hair length. Angela was older and dark, probably Italian or Greek, with thick bristling hair and burning eyes.

"I see he goes for all types," Nina said.

"He does."

"They ought to give out crosses when you get off the ferry, to ward him off."

"It wouldn't help. He has some sort of charm . . . I don't know how to describe it."

"How about Transylvanian?"

Cheryl's attention was suddenly diverted to the bar. "Let's get a drink," she said with urgency.

"Okay." That was abrupt, Nina thought. Was this a sign of a problem with alcohol?

Cheryl hustled her over to the punch bowl. "Sunmist is famous for their margarita punch," Cheryl said too loudly. Her voice caught the attention of a man off to the right. He turned toward them.

"Cheryl, hi." He touched her on the arm. Intimate, but less aggressive than one of Barry's elbow squeezes.

"Jonathan, how ya' doing?"

"Okay."

"You remember Nina, don't you? We ran into you this afternoon, on our way from the ferry to the house."

"Sure. Hi."

It was the man in the white cotton shirt. He had changed his outfit, but he was still wearing the same kind of shirt. This time it was blue, paired with khaki pants and a braided leather belt. He also wore deck shoes. He had a more formal look than the rest of the crowd, in their oversize jungle-print T-shirts, shorts, and beach sandals. Jonathan was overdressed in the simplest sense of the word—he was wearing too many clothes. Which could have made him look like just some tight-assed Upper East Sider not worth a second glance. One of those smug types that made Nina mutter under her breath, "Go back to Jim McMullen's." But Jonathan had an air of vulnerability that saved him from smugness. And Nina was always a sucker for an alienated preppy. It came from having read *Catcher in the Rye* over and over at an impressionably young age.

"Hi," she said. It sounded small, too monosyllabic for a party with margarita punch. "Nice to meet you again," she added, trying to sound a bit more raucous. And she gave herself what she hoped was an unobtrusive tug at her crotch.

"Same here."

Cheryl paused a moment, to see if the conversation was going to go anywhere, and then jumped in. "I dragged Nina out here for a week to see if she wanted to take Mindy's place. You heard about the Mindy debacle, didn't you?"

"I did."

"Jonathan's an old friend of Barry's."

"Oh." Nina nodded politely.

"But he's much nicer."

"That's me. Mr. Nice Guy."

"He was in our house last summer, but decided to move on."

"Nothing personal."

"I know." Cheryl turned to Nina. "Jonathan's house has some really interesting artwork. You should get him to show it to you."

That dump? Nina was surprised. The place they had stopped off at with all the dishes in the sink didn't exactly look like the Leo Castelli gallery. She hadn't noticed any artwork. "But didn't we—" she started, but then Cheryl stepped on her small toe.

"There's a woman in the house who sculpts," he said. "She brought out a few pieces. They're small but skillful, I think. I could show them to you if you were interested in that sort of thing."

If she was interested in what sort of thing? Sculpture? Or having him take her back to his house? In terms of the latter, she thought it a bit premature. As far as her feelings about sculpture went . . . well, that was a little more complicated.

She loved the Brancusi and Giacometti pieces in the museums. But she seemed to lack vision when it came to the stuff that was actually in people's living rooms. Sometimes she felt that art appreciation was something that was directly proportional to the socioeconomic level in which you had grown up. It seemed as though it was the Scarsdale girls who had the easiest time oohing and aahing. The Bronx girls often found it hard not to snicker.

Nina had worked hard against the snickering, schlepping all over Europe, immersing herself in Klimt and Brueghel in Vienna, Picasso in Barcelona, Matisse in Paris. Even hitchhiking out to Otterloo, hours from Amsterdam, to get a good dose of Van Gogh. And she had returned, convinced that she was a changed woman. But most of the time, whenever anyone showed her their private collections, she just didn't get it. The word *dreck* often came to mind.

Nina more than suspected that there was a subtle sociological subtext to this syndrome. Not only were the Scarsdale girls prone to majoring in art history, many of them had the actual audacity to go to art school. No one at Bronx Science had gone to art school. Nina and her friends were all packed off to premed, predent, and prelaw programs. A paintbrush or a chisel was considered a dangerous thing in the boroughs, an object that could distract you from Making a Living.

Other women lived with the fear of ending up in the street. Nina lived in fear of ending up in a loft with inadequate heat, driven half mad by a talent that wouldn't let go. As a result, Nina had a feeling that on the whole she might not be completely objective about art.

"Sculpture?" she said, smiling at Jonathan with what she hoped was a mixture of casualness and warmth. "I'm not rabid about it, but I know what I like."

"Since you'll be out all week, maybe you'll make it over there," he said.

"Jonathan's working on a commission basis," Cheryl added.

"She's kidding," he said quickly.

"What *do* you do?" Nina asked him.

A troubled look flickered across his eyes. "I'm in advertising." Well, there was certainly something going on here. He looked worried and his answer was vague. Nina had dated enough unemployed men in her time to recognize the signs. But at least he wasn't a lawyer. She hadn't had much luck with them lately. Like for the past ten years.

"Jonathan, how long are you staying out?" Cheryl asked.

"I'll be here for at least another week or two. I don't have to get the boat back until later on in the month, when my father goes on vacation. So I'd like to make use of it while I can. Barry and I are going out tomorrow, as a matter of fact."

"Yeah, he mentioned it to me," Cheryl said.

"Do you like sailing?" he asked Nina.

Oy vay, don't get me started, she said to herself. If you think I have a lot of class anger about sculpture, wait until you see me in the vicinity of a sailboat. "Sure," she said. The jumpsuit was creeping up on her again. This was the last time she'd let Cheryl give her fashion advice. She hoped the Red Queen hadn't misled her about this vacation as well.

Although so far she couldn't complain. The women in the house seemed nice enough. Those two men, whatever their names were, hadn't shown up yet. But no matter how awful they were, they'd be outnumbered. And Cheryl was bossy as always, but probably nothing Nina couldn't handle. Meanwhile this guy, this grown-up version of Holden Caulfield, looked like he had definite possibilities.

The only fly in the ointment so far was Barry Adelman. And Nina had a feeling, considering his schedule, she probably wouldn't be seeing too much of him.

CHAPTER 7

Nina woke later than usual the next morning. It was after ten and Cheryl was still asleep. She heard male voices coming from upstairs. Lying in bed for a while, Nina wondered what the dress code was. Should she just pop up there in her thin white cotton nightgown? Pretending that she wasn't even aware that the outline of her nipples and pubic hair were plainly visible? Or she could put on a robe, but bathrobes had problems all their own.

The idea of them was nice—casual but classy, very Depression-era screwball comedic. But the truth was that once you tied the belt at the waist, no matter how loosely, it looked like hell unless you were wearing a bra. And it seemed too contrived to put a bra on under your robe. Why not just put on all your clothes already? Robes without belts were out of the question, of course. Too Bronx.

Nina finally grabbed a robe and put it on over her nightgown. The belt was visible, thereby eliminating the Bronx factor, but remained untied, eliminating the sag factor. It was a compromise situation, but most things were.

A man sat on a stool at the breakfast bar in the kitchen area, reading the *New York Times*. He wore glasses and had a beard. The glasses had the wrong sort of frames, thick black Woody Allen ones, as if he were still a sophomore at Brooklyn Tech. The beard was shot with gray. The overall impression was nerdy. Shit, Nina murmured to herself, but she felt her body relax with relief.

"Hi. I'm Nina Fischman." She took his hand. She made sure her handshake was firm enough to compensate for her lingerie, which suddenly seemed to be flopping around in disarray. His handshake was a three-act play, with a tentative approach, a loxlike middle, and an intimate climactic squeeze. Nina loved happy endings. She felt herself warm toward him.

"Ira Mendelssohn," he said. "Charlie and I just came over on the nine o'clock ferry."

"I thought you guys were coming out last night."

"Yeah, well, we decided to go to the movies after work so we'd miss the rush hour. But by the time the film was over, we were too wiped to drive out. So we stayed in the city." She briefly wondered if they were a couple, but then dismissed the idea. Davis Park seemed to be homogeneously heterosexual.

It was amazing how provincial New Yorkers were when it came to their summer homes. They went running right back to their roots, either of ethnic or sexual preference. There they were, a mere fifty miles from the center of the city. A city where people mixed happily, taking great pride in leading lives of diversity. But come Memorial Day weekend, the gorgeous mosaic crumbled. Even the most sophisticated New Yorkers reghettoized themselves. The gays ran to the Pines or Cherry Grove, the WASPs to Nantucket or Shelter Island, the wealthy blacks to Sag Harbor, the Irish to Greene County or Breezy Point, and the Jews to Fair Harbor or Westhampton Beach. Davis Park at least seemed somewhat ethnically diverse, if not heterogeneous when it came to sexual preference.

"Are you here for the weekend?" Ira asked her.

"I'm going to be out for the week. Sharing a room with Cheryl."

"Oh, filling in for Mindy?" He laughed, but without meanness. "How's she doing?" he asked sympathetically.

"I don't know. I've never met her."

"I see. Coffee's ready. Want some?"

"Sure, thanks."

"Charlie, coffee," he called out to the deck.

A dark man came inside in response. "Yo," he said. He didn't look like the kind of man who should be saying yo. He looked like the kind of man who should be fitting Ira for eyeglasses.

"This is Nina," Ira said. "And this is Charlie Russo."

"Hello. No milk please."

"I know. Nina is Mindy's replacement."

"Really? How is Mindy?"

"I don't know," she repeated. "Cheryl and I work in the same office. I haven't really met too many of her friends. I don't think I remember anyone named Mindy. What was she like?" Suddenly she was curious.

"A tall, loud blonde," Charlie said. "You'd like her. She's lots of fun. Or was, anyway. Poor thing."

"You've been warned about him, I take it?" Ira asked.

"My God, there are no secrets in this place, are there?"

"People talk."

"Speaking of people," Nina said, "where is everyone?"

"My guess would be aerobics on the beach," Charlie said. "Is that where Cheryl is?"

"No, she's still asleep."

"She is? That's unusual. She's a hard-core aerobics head."

The phone rang. Ira picked it up. "Hello?" He paused. "Anybody seen Barry?"

"Nope," they both answered.

"No one's seen him," he said. He listened for a minute and then turned to Nina and Charlie. "He was supposed to meet Jonathan at the boat fifteen minutes ago. Charlie, you better check and see if he's still asleep."

"Okay." Charlie walked off in the direction of Barry's room.

"I'll bet he's not there," Nina said, remembering the strawberry blonde at the sunset party.

"You think he got lucky?" Ira asked.

"Doesn't he always?"

"You catch on fast," he said.

"People talk."

Charlie returned to the kitchen, the color drained from his face. He remained silent.

"So is he here?" Ira asked.

"Not exactly."

Ira shook his head in disgust. He handed Charlie the phone. "Here, you talk to him."

"Jonathan? Hi. It's Charlie. . . . Fine . . . Yeah, he's still in bed. Sort of. Actually, he's dead. In bed. Dead in bed," he repeated numbly.

Ira and Nina gasped.

"Y-yeah, I'm s-sure," Charlie continued, choking on the words. He turned to Ira. "Should Jonathan . . . um . . . call the police? Uh . . . or an ambulance or something?"

"Well, was he murdered?" Nina asked, having had experience with this sort of thing.

"Jesus Christ, I don't know. He's just dead. He doesn't have a knife sticking out of his stomach."

"Tell him to call the police."

"Okay, Jonathan, call the police, I guess," Charlie said. "We'll be here. We're not going anywhere." He hung up.

"Were you kidding or what?" Ira said.

"Do I look like I'm kidding? No, really, go take a look."

"Come with me."

"No, thanks. Once was enough."

"You?" Ira turned to Nina.

She thought about it for a minute. Nina might have had a fair amount of experience with untimely demises, but she had never been faced with a dead body before. "Maybe we should wait until the police come," she suggested weakly. "If there was foul play, we wouldn't want to mess up the crime scene."

"Foul play?" said Charlie. "I don't know."

"Well, how does he look?" Ira asked.

"Dead, very dead."

"Any blood?"

"No blood. He's just lying there, not breathing. I can't tell what happened," Charlie said.

"Is there anything over his mouth?" Ira asked.

"Like what?"

"Like a plastic bag?"

"Of course not."

"You sure?"

"Of course I'm sure. I'd have noticed. Ira, what do you think I am, an idiot or something?"

Nina interrupted their dialogue. "Did Barry have any disease that anyone knew about?"

"Just a permanently hard cock."

"Right," said Ira. "Charlie, did you check to see if it was still hard?"

"You don't believe me, do you?" said Charlie, looking like he was about to cry.

"I think I hear Cheryl," Nina said. The three of them exchanged looks as if they had a guilty secret. Cheryl emerged wearing nothing but a very large white T-shirt. Her thin tan legs made excellent accessories.

"Coffee?" she asked.

The men sat there mutely.

"What's wrong with everyone?" Cheryl snapped.

Nina took the plunge. "Barry's lying in his bed. And he's dead."

"Is he alone?" Cheryl asked.

"Yeah," said Charlie.

"Well, that's unusual," said Cheryl.

CHAPTER 8

Cheryl was fearless, as opposed to Charlie and Ira, who were relying upon the kitchen counter to hold them up. She marched right into Barry's room and stayed there. After a minute or two, Nina followed her in.

"What do you think?" Nina asked.

"I think he's dead." Cheryl's voice was steady.

"I guess I meant how did it happen."

"How should I know?"

"Do you think it was natural causes?"

"Well, he looks pretty natural, doesn't he?" He did. There was no evidence of trauma. Barry just lay there with his eyes closed, looking like he was sleeping off a Friday night that featured too much margarita punch. Except that he wasn't breathing.

"But it makes no sense. He wasn't sick or anything."

"I assume they'll do an autopsy," Cheryl said.

"I guess so." If anyone in the room was an expert on

murder, it was Nina. Yet she instinctively deferred to Cheryl. That bossiness—you either had it by the fourth grade or you lived your life without it. It wasn't something you could develop; it was as predetermined as juvenile diabetes.

She heard Jonathan come into the house. You could hear everything in this place. The walls were the thickness of emery boards. Jonathan trooped into the bedroom, along with Ira and Charlie. There was hardly space for the five of them. Barry's quarters, though a bit larger than the room Nina shared with Cheryl, were still a modest size. He kept the room sparsely furnished, most of the square footage being taken up by a pair of barbells. The only decoration was a James Dean poster tacked to the wall. Or it might have been the guy from *Beverly Hills 90210*. Nina couldn't really tell them apart. She was the wrong age for both, a member of the generation sandwiched between men who combed their hair back.

"When did he come in last night?" asked Jonathan, who didn't comb his hair back. Who probably didn't comb his hair at all. "Was he alone?"

"I don't think we know," Cheryl said. "Ira and Charlie didn't come out until this morning. And Nina and I must have been asleep by the time he got back."

"Anybody else see him? If I recall correctly, there are at least a hundred and thirty-seven other people who live in this house."

"It's not that crowded," Cheryl said. "You just caught an especially loud bunch last summer. And I don't know if anybody saw him. Where are they all, anyway?"

"Probably aerobics," Ira said.

"Jesus, what time is it?" Cheryl grabbed Jonathan's wrist and checked his watch. "It's late. After eleven. Nice watch, Jonathan." Boy, she sounded awfully cavalier for someone who was in a room with a corpse. Particularly a corpse she had previously been intimate with.

"Thanks. I got it for sailing."

"Oh, yeah. You and Barry were supposed to go out on the boat today, weren't you?"

"That's right."

At that moment, someone banged on the front door. "Anybody home?" The voice was male and middle-aged. Well, technically everyone in the house could qualify as middle-aged, if you used the standards that Nina adhered to as a kid. If this was the fifties, Nina would be old enough to be wearing a hat with a veil. But there was something old-fashionedly middle-aged about the voice. Not the voice of a guy who still rented shares in summer houses; it was the voice of a guy who bowled in a league and fished for blues on the weekend.

"Who's there?" Cheryl called.

"Suffolk County Police." The door banged as he let himself in.

"In here," Cheryl called again.

Two cops appeared. The middle-aged bowling bluefisherman was accompanied by a younger Al Pacino type. They attempted to enter the room, but one dead body and seven live ones were too much for the bedroom to hold. For a while it looked like the stateroom scene from *A Night at the Opera,* until the older cop told everyone to get out.

They retreated to the kitchen and huddled around the coffeepot, like survivors. No one spoke. Jonathan started to cry.

"Are you okay?" Nina asked him.

"Yeah, it's just . . . Christ, we went way back. I mean, we used to copy each other's homework in high school."

It was hard to imagine Barry and Jonathan growing up in the same neighborhood. Or on the same planet, for that

matter. Barry had the lean and hungry look of a male borough ethnic. Eyes narrowed and darting, constantly moving
forward. Or else, like a shark, you would die. Keep talking,
keep squeezing those elbows. All the boys were that way back
in Nina's elementary school. In perpetual motion, tapping
their pencils, throwing spitballs, poking each other in the
ribs. When Nina read studies later on that claimed boys aca-
demically dominated the classroom while girls just collapsed
into silent shrinking violets, it made her laugh. That wasn't
the way she remembered it. She was quite sure that most of
those boys never even learned to read. Nowadays they had
diagnoses—attention-deficit disorder, hyperkinesis, dyslexia,
and all that. Back then, there seemed to be nothing dysfunc-
tional about it. It was just part of the condition of being a
male child in an overcrowded New York City classroom. And
Barry had never outgrown it.

Jonathan, on the other hand, had the stillness of a deer
trapped by headlights. Speed was not his thing. How could
this man have grown up in a borough? He would have been
eaten alive. Nina considered pressing the matter, but Jonathan was still in tears and it seemed like an awkward time to
cross-examine him about his childhood.

Men in tears was something Nina had been brought up
to think was good, a positive sign. She had gone to college
during a time when the most desirable catches were the sensitive ones in men's groups who wore white drawstring pants.
And if you could get one to cry, that was really good. So as
the rest of the group nervously averted their eyes, Nina
stepped right up and snuggled in.

"You poor thing. I had no idea you two were so close."
She tried to summon up some feelings of sadness. But it was
hard getting past the feeling that Barry's death had been a
good thing, an attempt by a well-meaning exterminator to rid
the world of a mutational strain of odious vermin.

Under her close but well-meaning scrutiny, Jonathan stopped crying. The Al Pacino type police officer came out to use the phone. Everyone strained to listen, but the cop hunched into himself as he talked and kept his voice to an inaudible level. "Okay" was all they heard. He turned to them after he hung up. "You were right. He's dead."

"No kidding." Cheryl and Charlie said it simultaneously.

"I've got some paramedics coming to take him over to the mainland."

"I should call his mother," Jonathan said.

"Do you have her number?" Cheryl asked.

"No, but I could call directory assistance. Sylvia Adelman. But I can't remember which town she lives in. I used to know. It has the same name as some show tune. Barry always used to make a joke out of it. Now what could it be?"

"Gary, Indiana?" Charlie suggested.

"What would Mrs. Adelman be doing in Gary, Indiana? What do you think, she's a retired steelworker? She lives in Florida, of course."

"Sunrise," Cheryl said.

"Right. Barry would always run around singing "Sunrise, Sunset" whenever he had to go visit her."

"Hold on," the cop said. "We're going to have to question each of you."

Nina noticed that Jonathan had broken out in a sweat. She wondered if that should be considered suspicious. Until she noticed that she had broken out in a sweat also. It was getting hot and sticky in the house. She started to slip out of her robe when she remembered her transparency problem.

"Officer, can I get dressed?"

"Okay," he said, looking annoyed. Maybe she should ask him for a hall pass.

Nina went downstairs, took off her robe, and lay on her bed for a moment. Images swirled before her—the ferry ride, the sun, the piña coladas, the jumpsuit creeping up her crotch, the seven women giggling on the deck. And Barry's corpse, lying naked under a sheet, formed the centerpiece. It was dizzying, making her want to just lie there and pull the blanket up over her head. But it was too sticky for that. Besides, she had to pick out an outfit, one that was appropriate for a police investigation.

CHAPTER 9

Questioning was taking place simultaneously on the front and back decks, despite the threat of rain. Detective Connell, the beefy middle-aged one, seemed to be heading the investigation. But it was Detective Ferrari who ultimately called Nina out onto the rear deck.

He smiled and assured her that this was routine, that she wasn't a suspect, but that she was expected to cooperate fully. She assured him she would, and launched into an explanation of how she had just gotten there the day before, and that she was just having her morning coffee when Charlie stumbled upon Barry's body.

"Who was in the house at the time?" Ferrari asked.

"Just Charlie and Ira and me. Cheryl was asleep downstairs."

"And where was everybody else?"

"Down at the beach, taking an aerobics class."

"Who was down there?"

"Let me see." She knew there had been nine people in the house when they started out yesterday. Ira and Charlie made eleven. Nina kept trying, but she couldn't come up with six names. Right off the bat she could remember Harriet, the nice one, and Barbara, the one with the big mouth. After a while, she retrieved Maggie the Magpie and Nancy the red-head, but despite the mnemonic devices, she needed Ferrari's help to remember Estelle and Elizabeth.

It was only in the middle of the interrogation that it dawned on Nina that she herself would make an excellent suspect. After all, the house had been humming along nicely all through June, everyone treating one another with mutual respect, washing each other's dishes and making pots of coffee. Then Nina Fischman shows up and the next day someone's dead in his bed.

She made a likely suspect except for one thing. She had never even met Barry Adelman until Friday afternoon. Which gave her a mere twelve hours to develop a motive. Considering who he was, twelve hours would have been sufficient if she were prone to such things. Of course, she didn't mention that to Ferrari. On the other hand, she could have been a contract killer. He might have thought of that on his own. Just in case he did, she tried to act as unlike a contract killer as possible until he finished with her. She trotted out her rusty old sweet qualities, moldering from disuse during her years as a practicing attorney. As if she were on a blind date with a man who had been described as looking for someone nice.

After the police and the body had left, a queer stillness descended on the house. It reminded Nina of a September day she had spent in Fair Harbor during a hurricane watch. Meanwhile, the aerobics addicts had returned en masse, giggling and perspiring, and had been quickly hushed and questioned, one by one, by the police. Now they sat in the living room, still wearing sweaty bicycle shorts, gulping at their water bottles through built-in straws. And holding a wake, of sorts, for Barry Adelman.

The conversation was entertaining, but Nina was distracted by trying to remember everyone's name while they spoke. Harriet seemed the most upset. Which made sense since she was the nice one. Cheryl didn't seem too broken up. At first Nina found this surprising. But she had to admit to herself that if she were being totally honest, she'd probably want most of her ex-boyfriends dead. Especially the ones with good jobs who had gotten married and had children named Lily and Sophie and Jack. Maybe that was why Harriet could be emotionally expressive with her grief—no baggage. Or so Nina thought.

"You know who's really going to miss him?" Harriet asked, through tears that seemed genuine if not plentiful.

"Who?" snorted Maggie the Magpie with unhidden derision.

"The kids."

"You mean Jenny?" asked Barbara. "And that other teenager he seduced during the sunset party at the Pink House last month? And all those other mere children whose lives he touched?" She camped it up on the last three words so that you couldn't help thinking of everything else he touched.

"No, I meant the kids he taught. They were wild about him."

"They were?" Cheryl was clearly amazed.

"Sure, they thought he was better than MTV. You knew that, didn't you?"

"No, not really."

"You should have. You knew Barry better than any of us. Didn't he ever talk about school to you?"

"Actually, he never did. He probably discussed it with you because of your background."

"I'm a guidance counselor," Harriet explained to Nina. "But I'm thinking of becoming a veterinarian."

It made sense. If the kids in your class acted like animals, it must be tempting to go for the real thing.

"Well, I, for one, am shedding no tears," said Elizabeth, directing a stray wisp of hair away from her regal forehead. "I can't believe how many of you succumbed. I never let him touch me."

"Who *do* you let touch you?" asked Barbara, the one without discretion. The one who Nina had judged to be the most fun.

"Now, Barbara," said Nancy, the good-looking redhead, "you know perfectly well that Elizabeth is in a long-distance relationship."

"A long-distance relationship," Barbara repeated, giving the words an earnest, journalistic reading, making the entire concept sound ridiculous. "With a museum curator in San Francisco." She extended her pinky the tiniest bit, just enough to remind her audience of the stereotypical connotations associated with Bay Area art historians.

They were all decent enough to ignore her, but Nina felt bad for Elizabeth anyway. Not that she had anything in common with the well-bred, thin, quiet, poised woman wearing an outfit composed of various shades of cream. But Nina had, after all, spent her childhood as a schoolteacher's daughter among the offspring of cab drivers and grocery clerks. And although no one stuck their pinkies out when she passed by, the things they said had come close enough. So she knew how Elizabeth felt. But she had also often been the only borough girl in a roomful of expensive private-school educations. There were probably roomfuls of people that would make even Elizabeth feel like a guttersnipe. It was all relative.

Elizabeth turned to Barbara and said, with quiet dignity, "Yes, that's right. Roger's living in San Francisco now."

A very classy reply. One that cut her off right at the knees. "Well," Barbara snapped, trying to regain her footing, "I'm not ashamed to admit that I slept with him. Twice, as a matter of fact."

"And how was he?" asked Maggie.

"As if you didn't know."

"Who, me?" Maggie put her hand to her throat in mock innocence and fluttered her eyelids.

"Cut the crap." Cheryl pushed up her sleeves as if she were really getting down to business. "Let's get it over with and go around the room, shall we?"

"Good idea," Barbara said.

"Easy for you two," said Nancy. "You've already made your disclosure. Now you want to drag the rest of us down with you."

"Yeah," said Estelle. "That's just like s-someone who's been s-swimming laps in cold water yelling 'Everybody into the pool.'"

It was a good analogy. Nina gave Estelle a closer look. She hadn't really noticed her before. The woman was so quiet. But upon further inspection, there was an air of intelligence about her. Especially about her hair. She was paying the right person a great deal of money to cut it. Estelle seemed to have a slight stutter, which might explain why she wasn't heard from more often. In this crowd, the slightest lack of fluency put you at a distinct disadvantage.

"All right," said Harriet. "I'll go next. I admit it. I slept with him." That was a real conversation stopper. All eyes had been turned toward Nancy, who they expected to confess next. Harriet's admission caused necks to snap.

"Why in the world did you ever do that?" Cheryl asked.

"For the same reason everybody else in this room did. Because I felt like it."

"Not *everybody* in this room," Elizabeth said.

"Right. Not Nina," said Barbara.

"What are you implying?" asked Elizabeth.

"I'm implying that I've seen you in bed with Barry."

"That doesn't mean anything."

"It must mean s-something," Estelle said.

"Oh, please," Elizabeth said. "That hardly counts. We were just messing around a little one afternoon. Nothing happened. I mean, we didn't have intercourse or anything."

"Elizabeth is impenetrable," Barbara explained.

"Well, I had intercourse with him," Nancy said. "Five times."

"Four for me," Maggie said.

"The man would fuck a knothole in a pine board," Estelle said. "I s-slept with him a couple of times."

"How many?"

"I lost count."

"In the double digits?"

"I don't know."

"It's probably in the double digits if you lost count."

"Maybe."

"When did all this take place?" asked Nina.

"During the week, I bet," said Elizabeth. "When no one was looking."

"During aerobics classes," Maggie said. "It was the perfect opportunity. Everyone else was down on the beach. I viewed it as an alternative form of exercise."

"One thing I'll give him credit for," Nancy said. "He always used a condom. I appreciated that."

"Oh, yeah." Cheryl sounded contemptuous. "Barry and his condoms. He made a big thing about it, like he was the most enlightened man in the world. Meanwhile, it was just another one of his gimmicks, another way to impress women and get them into bed."

Nina knew what she meant. It was like the feminist-man

syndrome during college. On her campus there had always been a strong contingent of undergraduate males who relied upon calling themselves feminists in order to get laid. Condom use was the recent equivalent. It constituted a historical change, however, for condoms used to be seedy little things, never in wide use in Nina's generation. Who needed them, with all the IUD's, diaphragms, pills, and cervical caps that filled the dresser drawers of Nina's dormitory. Condoms receded into obscurity, attaining status as a cultural oddity, like drinking hard liquor or voting for Ike. And then, just like vodka and the Republican Party, they made a big comeback. And heterosexual men who had never previously had the opportunity to unwrap one in their youth started acting like condoms were the harbingers of a new age of enlightenment. And the fact that they put a sock on without *kvetching* about it made them veritable Renaissance men. Nina was sure that Barry Adelman was a prime example of this syndrome.

"What a bunch of sluts." Charlie came in from the deck, where he had apparently been listening to every word.

He was kidding, but Nina was glad she didn't have to be counted in. She wondered whether she would have gone down like everyone else. Probably. The man had obviously been good at what he did.

CHAPTER 10

Fire Island is a quiet place. No cars, no trains, just the occa-sional whir of an industrial-strength blender and the soft murmur of voices spreading gossip. By early evening, everyone knew more about Barry's death than the *Newsday* reporter covering the story.

Barry had been poisoned. Nina had heard it from Cheryl, who had heard it from someone who heard it from one of the guys who worked on the ferry and was supposedly the brother of a Suffolk County police officer. It wasn't exactly clear how he had been poisoned or with what. And certainly not at all clear by whom. But speculation had taken over like a tenacious weed, choking all other topics of conversation.

Meanwhile, the poisoning angle had elevated Barry to the status of folk hero, up from town tramp. People couldn't talk enough about him, couldn't get sufficient obscure details, as if the entire town of Davis Park had been assigned to cover the story of Barry Adelman's life for *People*. Right this minute, out on the deck, Jonathan Harris was regaling a small crowd with stories of Barry's junior year in high school. And people were practically taking notes, as if they were on the front desk instead of the front deck. Jonathan was doing a good job of it, too, combining the style of a cynical raconteur with just the right amount of tender pathos.

"Only Barry could have pulled it off," he reminisced. "Not only did Mrs. Wasser pass him, but she let him be on the French squad the following year."

"What the hell does the French squad do?" asked Barbara. "Patrol the halls for bad accents?"

"I don't know," said Jonathan. "Probably spend three study periods a week sucking up to Mrs. Wasser."

"And I bet Barry was a master suck-up," Barbara said. "Especially when it came to women teachers."

"He was a master suck-up in the sense that he could do it without making you sick. It wasn't as if he'd come on all gushy and fawning. But he'd sort of look you levelly in the eye, letting you know that he knew that you knew that he was conning you, and proceed from there. He conned you with dignity. You never felt violated afterward. You just felt like you had negotiated a transaction with a superb businessman, someone who had earned his share of the deal."

"It sounds like you spent a fair amount of time on the other side of the table," Cheryl said.

"I did. I did indeed." Jonathan gave a wistful smile and added a small self-deprecatory roll of his eyes that caught Nina's attention. He was pretty good with the self-deprecation routine for someone who wasn't a Jew. Or maybe he was.

She had hypersensitive antennae when it came to self-deprecation. It was the language of her childhood, her mother tongue, a dialect that had been transplanted from the shtetl to the boroughs virtually intact. At Bronx Science they had tried to teach a new language, that of taking yourself seriously. Apparently it had taken hold for many in her graduating class, for when Nina had forced herself to go to her twentieth-year reunion last spring, she had found accountants and lawyers and heart surgeons who talked earnestly about their curricula vitae without once letting their eyeballs drift even the slightest bit upward. Meanwhile, she still shrugged and shuffled and rolled her eyes like mad, letting her voice naturally fall into a question mark at the end of every sentence. The heart surgeon alumni all seemed to keep a well-modulated tone, ending their sentences right at the place they began them. She remembered them as sophomores, pimply and short, with voices that cracked and wavered all over the place. How had they learned to talk like Episcopalians? She was an anachronism like Henry Kissinger, who had come to this country at a relatively young age and had done everything right—gone to Harvard, landed a good job, married a tall, blond Christian—and still couldn't shake the guttural accent of his early German childhood.

So when she saw Jonathan roll his eyes, she felt as though it was a signal for her to respond. The way a Jew will casually slip a Yiddish word into the conversation, to establish that both conversers are indeed members of the tribe. And the other person will give a little nod or smile of acknowledgment. Or even use that same word or another Yiddish word, giving it a pronunciational flourish that leaves no doubt that you're listening to a native speaker.

Except that Jonathan was looking at Cheryl, not Nina. And ordinarily it was bad etiquette to throw yourself into the middle of a male-female exchange while eye contact was still being maintained. Not bad etiquette exactly, but it did make you look somewhat like a desperate loser. However, there was something about Jonathan that made Nina feel like it was okay to butt in. And Cheryl had already dismissed him as far as her sexual interests went. What was it she had said about him? Too mammalian for her tastes. He seemed very mammalian—warm-blooded and fuzzy, with a small layer of subcutaneous fat that made Nina want to press her fingers into his belly to see how far they'd sink in.

"I spent a lot of time on the other side of the table," Jonathan said. "Several decades. And I wish that I could say he never done me wrong."

"But you can't," Nina said.

Jonathan shifted his gaze to her. "No, I can't."

Nina launched into the question that had been on her mind all afternoon. "What were you two doing in the same high school anyway? You must have been the Brother from Another Planet. Like Cathy on the old *Patty Duke Show.* Were you doing your junior year abroad or something?"

"Bayside High School had all different types back then. Kids like me, who grew up in big old houses in Douglaston Manor. And kids like Barry, from garden apartments in Deepdale. And everyone in between." Jonathan leaned forward. "It was a big school. Later they built Cardozo, which siphoned off our younger brothers and sisters. But even there you had both sides of the Douglaston tracks mixing it up."

It helped place his age. Too old to have gone to Benjamin Cardozo High School. She wasn't exactly sure when the place had opened, but she had known people at college who had graduated from there. Which made Jonathan older than she. That was less intimidating. She knew that many women her age had taken to cruising the ranks of the latter half of the baby boom. Younger men were developing a reputation for having fewer commitment problems, for being less sexist, less neurotic in general.

They made Nina nervous. She always had the feeling that these well-adjusted twenty-nine-year-old guys would be repelled by her neuroses, the way they might be put off by graying hair or a bit of flab hanging from an upper arm. While someone who had spent their impressionable adolescence listening to the Kings and Queens of Neurotic Behavior (like Bob Dylan, Laura Nyro, and James Taylor) was more likely to give a neurotic personality proper respect. Jonathan looked like someone who worshiped at the altar of self-doubt. But in an attractive way.

"Barry was from Little Neck?" she asked.

"Jackson Heights originally. Then his family moved out there when Deepdale Gardens was built."

"I can't picture it somehow. He just doesn't seem like he grew up in a garden apartment complex." Actually, he seemed like he had sprung fully formed from the head of some oversexed Roman god.

"So what kind of wrong did Barry do you?" asked Cheryl.

Jonathan's eyes narrowed, perhaps with fear or embarrassment. "Do you have a few hours?"

"No, really," Cheryl insisted. "Tell us."

"All the stuff that you would imagine."

"Borrowing cars?"

"Yeah. And returning them with empty gas tanks and smashed headlights."

"What else?"

"Borrowing everything. And never returning anything."

"Like what?"

"Everything. Bikes, baseball cards, *Mad* magazines. And later on—along with the cars—records, stereo equipment, sweaters, leather jackets."

"And girlfriends?" Cheryl asked.

"What is this, a public humiliation?"

"What's the matter, don't you believe in full and fair disclosure?"

"Why don't you lay off—" Nina began, but Jonathan cut her off.

"What do you think?" he asked Cheryl. "Do you think Barry ever stole one of my girlfriends?"

"I'd put money on yes."

"Then you'd be a winner."

"Hmmm." Cheryl looked triumphant. And a little bit mean.

"That was a sucker bet," Nina said.

"What can I say?" Jonathan shrugged. "He was unbeatable. It has always been my private opinion that he even slept with Mrs. Wasser."

"The French squad lady?"

"Yeah. She used to get a funny look in her eye whenever Barry was around."

"How did you put up with it all these years?" Cheryl asked. "Why didn't you just dump him?"

"Why didn't you?" Jonathan asked her.

Good one, Nina thought. Jonathan Harris looked vulnerable and neurotic and was probably a major contender in the International Anhedonia Olympics. But he was not dumb.

Cheryl shifted her attention to a toenail whose polish was chipping. After half a minute of picking at it, she stood up. "I think it's time for piñas, don't you?" she said to no one in particular, and went inside.

CHAPTER 11

"I'm thinking of going to my sister's house," Nina said later that day. "I could catch a train at Patchogue out to West-hampton Beach."

"Why would you want to do that?" asked Cheryl.

"Frankly, it's a little bit creepy around here, in case you hadn't noticed. I feel like I'm at a wake."

"If you went to your sister's, you'd feel like you were at your own wake."

"It's not that bad."

"Nina," Cheryl said sternly. Nina recognized that voice. It was worse than the Red Queen. It was a Red Queen goes to Housing Court kind of voice. "You know damn well it certainly is that bad. And I'm only quoting you. None of this is based on personal observation, so don't get offended."

"I won't." Nina never did. Offended wasn't in her personal realm of human emotions. Depressed, paranoid, jealous, filled with despair—these were all everyday occurrences.

But you had to be at least a little self-righteous to get offended. And Nina had a depressed level of self-righteousness. Now, Cheryl was another story. There was someone who could get offended with the greatest of ease.

"Look," Cheryl went on, "every time you see your sister, you always come back acting like a dejected wreck. And the whole office has to spend the entire morning pumping up your self-esteem just to get it back to a level where you can function. Which is not what the taxpayers are paying for. It's a dreadful waste of human resources. And that's after only a one-night stand in Park Slope. Think of what a week in Westhampton Beach would do to you. I'm certainly not up to the task of resurrecting you. We'd have to call a psychiatric social worker into the office to perform crisis intervention. And quite frankly, what with the cuts and all, I'm not really sure we have the budget for it."

Nina laughed, but it wasn't funny. Her sibling relationship had just gotten worse and worse over the years. Nina used to rely on Laura as ballast to keep up her spirits. They were a balancing act, the two sisters. Nina with her conflicts and ambivalence, Laura with her rosy optimism, even if it bordered on the narrow and selfish. Nina used to feel that she could learn something from her younger sister, who seemed to have escaped the family curse of never feeling luckier than the most needy, wretched individual within the five boroughs (people in Iowa didn't count).

Laura had never been the one with red diaper rash. Even as young children, the older was the producer and the younger the consumer. And that had never changed. Nina displayed her intellect on the SAT's and letters to the *Times*, while Laura displayed her own sort of brilliance with her social agility and an earring collection that was worthy of a retrospective at the American Craft Museum. And Laura looked out for herself gracefully, without even seeming to display greed or callousness. Nina had always found it inspiring.

When had it changed? With the birth of Danielle, perhaps. Or maybe even earlier, with the marriage to Ken. Whatever. It didn't really matter precisely when it had happened, but over the past decade, Nina had felt excluded from Laura's inner circle.

Nina understood the necessity of this, as Laura's family increased. Only a madwoman or a saint could maintain an unlimited number of relationships of primary importance. Nina had been bumped back at each major family event. Looking at it in astronomical terms, she felt like she had started out as Mercury, or at least Venus, and was now hovering somewhere between Uranus and Neptune. Headed undoubtedly for post-Pluto obscurity.

But it was a natural progression. Anyone with three children had to be self-absorbed in order to survive. And Nina knew she was somewhat at fault herself. It was hard not to be hypersensitive in the face of the brownstone and the tennis-playing doctor husband and all the Shaker furniture out at the beach house. And the three perfect physical specimens that Ken and Laura had produced, each kid managing to look all-American without looking Christian. Danielle, Jared, and Evan all had the merest hint of kink to their hair and a slight generosity of nose that made them candidates for Jewish American Poster Children. They signaled hope that the race would survive without having to rely on the Satmars in Williamsburg with their heavy wool coats smelly with sweat from the summer heat.

The whole thing was a setup; Nina and Laura were inevitably poised for alienation, though Nina couldn't help but feel that her sister went just too far. She knew that Laura was bound to sound distracted at times and couldn't help but find Nina's never-ending man problems to be tedious, like a summer rerun you just can't sit through again. But Nina also knew herself to be a basically untedious person. And if all her plots seemed to evidence a dull sameness . . . well, she tried to make up for it in the presentation. However, no matter how hard she tried to be witty, how frantically she verbally tap-danced, she was no longer capable of getting Laura's attention. Whenever Nina used a sentence with *I* in it, her sister's mind went elsewhere.

And Laura at the beach was at her worst. Nina couldn't stand it. Everything was so perfect. The endless processions of Ball jars filled with dried crapola, lined up on the kitchen windowsill next to an equally endless procession of fruit preserves. Nina felt like she was choking on it all, the pepper jelly, the juniper berries, the dill weed, the dill salt, the homemade dill pickles. And the monotonous conversation about which tablecloth to use, which vase, which herb, which wine.

On the other hand, some instinct was telling Nina to get out of Davis Park. Westhampton Beach might not represent the pinnacle of emotional health, but at least it was devoid of homicide. She picked up the phone and dialed Laura.

Her sister answered on the fourth ring. "Hello?" She was a little breathless. Not the kind from anxiety, but from tennis or weeding.

"It's Nina. How ya doing?"

"Great." And she meant it too. "How are you?"

But Nina wasn't going to be tricked into answering. She knew better than to use a sentence with *I* in it. "You'll never believe what happened here," Nina said, and sailed into a description of the demise of Barry Adelman.

Her sister showed a little more interest than usual, but she remained restrained. "Imagine that," she said. When had Laura started sounding like an Episcopalian? Next she'd be exclaiming "indeed" instead of "holy shit."

"So I was thinking of getting the hell out of here," Nina

explained. "And thought I might drop in on you guys for a while."

"That would be fine. But I want to warn you. Joel and Sandy and their kids are out here. They're staying until Tuesday."

That killed that idea. Joel was Ken's partner and nice enough, but his wife was another story. Her attitude toward Nina varied between pity (since, as far as Sandy was concerned, there was nothing worse than an unmarried Jewish woman with unfirm thighs) and rage (since she couldn't understand why Nina wouldn't Just Do Something with Herself). And Nina would rather spend a week locked in a room staring at Barry Adelman's open casket than spend five minutes chatting with Sandy Slotnick.

"Good-bye," she told Laura. "I'll see you in the city."

"Don't be silly. Come out anyway. We're going to the lobster pound this afternoon. It'll be fun."

"Having Dr. Slotnick's wife watch me eat a lobster is not my idea of a good time."

"Oh, she's not that judgmental. It's all in your head."

"She's not judgmental when it comes to morons who can only discuss how to get to the Donna Karan outlet in Carlstadt, New Jersey. But try explaining how you simply cannot afford a week at Canyon Ranch no matter how much of a priority you make it, and then see how judgmental she can be."

"Okay, suit yourself. Is there really a Donna Karan outlet in New Jersey?"

"Ask Sandy."

"What are you going to do instead of coming out here?"

"I might go back to the city."

Cheryl must have overheard her. The voice of the Red Queen came from across the room. "Stop being ridiculous.

Don't even think about it. You said you'd spend the week and you're going to."

"Um, I think I'm staying," Nina said to Laura. Jesus, she thought, it was too much to deal with Cheryl and Laura simultaneously. Sometimes women could be worse than men.

CHAPTER 12

By the following morning, Nina had begun to reevaluate her decision. The rain, which had been threatening on and off since Friday night, had begun to take itself more seriously and the eleven of them—whoops, make that ten—were trapped inside, starved for entertainment. Several, including Nina, were playing around with an old game of Trivial Pursuit.

It was a game she could never win. Not that she didn't always make an excellent start, getting wedges like mad, putting to use all the mindless dreck she'd been carrying around in her head for decades. But she could never get the sports wedge. It was continually frustrating, sitting there with five wedges for an hour while everyone else caught up and then passed her by. It reminded Nina of her plight as a late-twentieth-century New York City woman. You could be smart, articulate, pretty, kind, intuitive, and ambitious. But if you weren't thin, you couldn't win. Thin was Nina's sports wedge.

This particular game was a little different. They were playing in teams and Ira, her partner, had assured her that he had no problem getting the orange wedge. He looked a little nerdy to be a sports freak, but so far he had done okay. The category was actually called Sports and Leisure and several of the questions had turned out to be about card games, which Ira knew a lot about. He had been Hearts champion in his college dorm for two years running.

They were losing, however, since Estelle had turned out to be a truly expert player, stammering out all the right answers before anyone else had even digested the question. Nina congratulated herself on yesterday's correct diagnosis of Estelle's intellect. Especially since Nina had initially based it solely on her haircut.

Except for Estelle, everyone played somewhat spiritlessly, since they had been playing with the same set for almost a decade. And all the questions sounded familiar. Not always familiar enough to remember the answers, but familiar enough to take the challenge out of the game. The later editions, baby boomer and such, had never caught on.

Nina and Ira had a choice between landing on a blue and a green square. It was a tough call for her, since geography and science were her best categories. Not because she was particularly good at them. And not because she was particularly bad at the others. She knew as much garbage about James Fenimore Cooper and Lucille Ball and Richard Nixon as most people. But most people, while able to recall endless details about sitcoms from *I Love Lucy* to Watergate, were hopeless when it came to map reading and the periodic table of the elements. In fact, Nina generally considered her education an inferior one, except when she watched someone else struggling on a green or blue square.

They decided to go for the blue, since it took them closer to a wedge they needed. Elizabeth read them their geography question. "What state is Mammoth Cave National Park located in?"

"Kentucky," Nina said right off the bat. "I'm sure of it," she added somewhat apologetically.

"Okay, we'll go with it." Ira had been quite good-natured throughout Nina's constant blurting out of the answers.

"Correct," Elizabeth said. "Speaking of mammoth caves, does anyone know how long the police are going to keep Barry's bedroom sealed?"

"What does Barry's bedroom have to do with mammoth caves?" Estelle asked. "It's not even big. At least as far as I can recall. I must admit, it's been a while since I checked."

"It loomed large in the imagination of many people," Elizabeth said.

"Well, I haven't heard anything about them unsealing the bedroom," Ira said. "But I did hear something interesting about Kim."

"Who's Kim?" asked Estelle. Everyone came to attention. Nina put down the dice, Elizabeth put down the card she'd been reading from. Cheryl put down the book she'd been reading across the room on the couch.

"That girl he was with at Sunmist," Ira answered.

"Woman," Estelle corrected.

"Girl," Ira insisted. "How old do you think she was?"

"Well, it's not clear that she had attained her majority," Nina said, venturing her legal opinion.

"Anyway, what did you hear about her?" Elizabeth asked.

"That the police are questioning her. And that she spent last Friday night on the Island, but it's not clear where."

"Who is she anyway?" Estelle asked. "I'd never s-seen her before."

"She's a Chogie," Ira said. It was the local term for townie, someone from Patchogue, where the ferry docked.

"And she was the last person s-seen with Barry?"

"She was," Ira said. "They apparently left the party together at about ten."

"Very interesting. And what else do you know about her?"

"Nothing. Just that the police are questioning her. And that she didn't go back to Patchogue that night, but that she claims she didn't spend the night with Barry. They're checking on that."

"She's certainly a good suspect," Nina said. "No one's ever seen her before. She appears out of nowhere, then disappears into the night with Barry and the next thing you know, he's dead."

"Please. Spare me." It was Cheryl from the couch.

"You don't like the Kim theory?" Nina asked.

"It stinks. First of all, she had no motive."

"To know Barry was to want to kill him," Elizabeth said. "Maybe he seduced and then dumped her, all in the space of a few hours. He surely was capable of it."

"So she poisoned him?" Cheryl said. "Come on. She just happened to be carrying around a toxic substance that she managed somehow to introduce into his system? No way."

"Maybe she was a serial killer," Ira said. "And she cruised sunset parties, just looking for men to murder."

"Look," Cheryl said. "The fact that it was poison makes it clear that the murderer was someone who already knew Barry. Poison is not indicative of impulse homicide."

"Maybe Kim did know him," Nina said. "Maybe she'd been harboring a grudge for years and was just waiting for the right opportunity."

"She wasn't old enough to have known him for years. Unless she was one of his junior high school students. And she didn't look like she'd last long in Bushwick," Ira said.

"She didn't know him," Cheryl said.

"How do you know?"

"I could tell by the way Barry was acting that he'd just met her."

"How could you tell?"

"He was buzzing around her in his frenetic way," Cheryl said. "The way he got right after he first caught scent of someone. With him, the effect wore off after thirty minutes. By the second hour of your acquaintance, he'd already be distracted, treating you like an old shoe."

Estelle laughed. "He had an adult attention deficit when it came to women. I wonder if the psy-psychologists can test for that. If they can, maybe we should have all our prospects give us their results before we get too involved."

"Cheryl, you seem like quite an expert when it comes to Barry Adelman," Elizabeth said.

"I've certainly had an opportunity to observe him over the years. I knew him well."

"Then according to your theory," Ira said, "you'd make an excellent suspect."

"But I wouldn't have used poison," Cheryl said. "I would have hacked him into little pieces. Very slowly."

"I sense a little hostility here," Ira said.

"I'm just kidding. I didn't hate him. Barry and I understood each other. Although I did get a little pissed at him about Mindy. But I warned her before she even set foot in this town. She walked right into that one."

"Ah, yes. Mindy," Ira said. "Does anyone know where Mindy was Friday night?"

"Mindy never struck me as the murderous type," Elizabeth said. "She was too good-natured."

"But she certainly overreacted to the Barry episode," Estelle said. "I mean, what was the big deal? He s-slept with her, he dumped her, it happened to all of us. We got over it. I would say her reaction was an indication of instability. Highly s-suspicious."

"Stop it," Cheryl said. "You're wrong and it's that movie that's to blame."

"What movie?"

"*Fatal Attraction.* It warped the minds of the American public. Women very rarely kill. If you knew anything about crime, you'd know that your typical murderer in a case like this would be someone who knew the victim a very long time and was desperate to get Barry out of their life."

"For what reason?"

"For whatever reason. Blackmail, for example."

"That's a good motive," Elizabeth said. "Now, who was Barry blackmailing?"

"No one," said Ira.

"How do you know?"

"Because if he was blackmailing someone, he wouldn't still be driving a beat-up old Chevy Nova with no sex appeal that he had to park all the way the hell over on a pier in the Hudson River because he couldn't afford the monthly fees on a lot east of Eleventh Avenue."

"As a matter of fact," said Cheryl, "he was planning on buying a new car. This fall."

"Really?" asked Ira. "He never mentioned it to me. And we used to talk about cars a fair amount."

"Maybe he didn't want to jinx it. But he certainly mentioned it to me."

"What kind?" Ira sounded dubious.

"A Honda. Accord, I think."

"Not possible. The Hondas didn't appeal to him. If he was going to go Japanese, he would have gotten a Camry. He liked the way they looked. And as we all know, looks were important to Barry."

"Anybody want to finish this game?" asked Estelle.

"Okay." Ira picked up the dice and rolled. "Yellow or brown? Your choice, Nina."

She wasn't in the mood for either Art and Literature or History. And it looked like it was clearing up out there. She had an urge for some solitude. She also wanted to get away from the sealed bedroom, which was sending off ghostly vibrations. She got up from the table. "Cheryl, want to take my place? I need to take a walk."

"I guess so. Or maybe I'll go with you. Which way are you heading?"

It took a few seconds for Nina to remember that she didn't have to answer. "I don't know," she said, only after she had stepped out onto the deck. The last thing she wanted was Cheryl's company. As she kept walking, she heard Cheryl telling Ira in that voice of hers about how Barry had become disillusioned with Toyotas in general and what he really wanted was a Saab.

Nina could picture Barry in a Saab, especially a convertible. She was sure that Barry could have pictured himself in one also. Was he blackmailing somebody? It wasn't outside the realm of possibility. Or maybe the murder was drug-related. She hadn't seen any evidence of drug use in the house, but that also was not outside the realm of possibility. He could have been up to his knees in cocaine. She tried to remember whether he seemed to have any trouble with his nose. Not that it meant anything these days, when people were consuming cocaine through other orifices and intravenous heroin use was making a middle-class comeback. She wondered exactly what the police had found before they sealed his bedroom.

CHAPTER 13

Nina headed east, toward Watch Hill. She decided to take the boardwalk instead of the beach, since she didn't feel like carrying her shoes. And she didn't dare go back to the house to drop them off in case Cheryl decided to accompany her.

Watch Hill was a marina and a campground run by the feds. She'd camped there when she was younger, with girl-friends and with Grant. Grant was the object of Nina's ambivalent affections for years, consuming the entire first half of Nina's thirties. They'd done a lot of camping together. At first Nina was very gung ho about the camping. And about Grant. But she'd gotten fussier as time went on, graduating from a foam pad to an air mattress and eventually insisting on a motel. Grant could never rise to the occasion of a motel and eventually the relationship ended.

Nina heard that he had gotten involved with a twenty-nine-year-old, which was the age Nina was when she met him. She was sure that Grant was giving whoever she was the grand tour of feeless camping grounds and day hikes that you could take a bus to. And that when this young woman got tired of foam pads and Short Line buses, he'd move on to another twenty-nine-year-old.

Or maybe not. Maybe he had met someone who could maintain a tolerance for foam pads forever and Grant would mate for life. She wished him well. She could afford to, for there was no bitterness or jealousy in her heart. Every day she woke up thankful that she was no longer involved with Grant Miller.

Instead she had gotten herself involved with Tom Wilson, who was outdoorsy without being cheap. Sometimes she didn't think she had made much progress. Instead of buses, she found herself on skimobiles and in four-wheel-drive vehicles. But they were still sleeping in a tent, albeit a four-hundred-dollar one that didn't leak. And she was still always cold and lately her back was starting to bother her. Maybe she should be on the lookout for one of those sixtyish divorcés who wore gold watches and took you to Boca for the weekend.

Would she really rather be in Boca than here? Now that the skies were clearing and she had gotten away from Cheryl's Red Queen voice, she was able to concentrate on how beautiful the place was. As Nina caught her first glimpse of Watch Hill, the dunes rising on the right and the boats bobbing in the bay to the left, she felt a tiny manic surge of exhilaration. It was a rare feeling. She only felt this way when walking. And she had to be alone and the scenery had to be good (Riverside Drive and upper Madison could usually do it for her) and she had to be not carrying a pocketbook. No matter how good the scenery, she never felt this way with her Coach tote on her shoulder.

She never seemed to get to do any serious walking anymore. Her first decade back in New York had been devoted to long-distance treks. If she had to be in the Village and it was a nice day, she'd consider leaving an hour and a half early to avoid the subway. Now she just ran around, from the dry cleaner to work to the gym, jumping in cabs, hopping on buses, catching subway trains. Trying to get from one place to the next in the shortest possible time.

She had wanted a more complicated life. She was still fleeing from memories of a childhood locked in a bedroom reading and a college career that took place almost entirely within the confines of her dorm room. Being bored and having nothing to do were early anxieties that she had overcompensated for. And it was exciting—having a boyfriend who required a serious commute, friends who required constant attention, a job that required her to actually think. But sometimes she missed the early Manhattan days when the hours stretched out before her and she'd slip her keys and a couple of bucks in her pocket and take off for distant zip codes.

Certainly the opportunities for purseless strolling had diminished. But now was one of those privileged times when Nina had an unbroken stretch of superb scenery in front of her and no handbag. She started to feel herself relax in a profound way. She imagined toxic, stress-related chemicals pouring out of her cells into her excretory system for disposal. Her endocrinologic balance shifted and she was sure she could feel the surge of serotonin and other happy, friendly secretions. Her spine realigned itself into a sturdier arrangement and her defenses, so multitudinous and constant that she was hardly aware of them, began to pop like soap bubbles on a surface. She felt open, ready to be filled up, able to handle anything.

"Where are you off to?" Jonathan appeared out of nowhere. "Escaping from the great privilege of sharing your space with so many interesting and lively people?"

"Well, actually, yes. That's exactly what I'm doing. Escaping. Especially from Cheryl." She knew it was inappropriate even before she said it. But Nina didn't care. She felt that gossip was one of life's great pleasures. It was more than a pleasure, really. It was a necessity. Talking about people was her major method of communicating. Nothing else held her interest in the same deep and passionate way. Sometimes she could get it up for a limited discussion about politics or movie stars or a book she'd read. And clothing was a topic that could sustain her interest for a good while. During one of her manic dieting phases, she was usually good for at least half an hour on vegetables. But mostly her great love was to sit back, relax, and discuss to death the cracks and crevices of the personality of a mutual acquaintance.

In general, men were not as good at this as women were. Their attention often wandered off after a few sentences, or else they started to look guilty. Some of them wouldn't even take the bait to begin with, just shrugging and saying "I don't know about that" and changing the subject. So Nina monitored Jonathan's response carefully to see which direction he'd take.

"Yeah, Cheryl." He smiled. "There's a real piece of work for you." It was a promising start.

"Well, I guess I knew what I was getting into," she said. "I mean, I have to work with the woman every day. I knew she was a tad bossy."

"Just a tad. You know, I was in that house last summer. I could have warned you. She's impossible. I used to go for long walks constantly. I'd come down here to Watch Hill and then walk back past Davis Park to Water Island. Then back to the house, take a leak, eat some lunch, and start all over again. Back and forth. I paced the whole season away, just to get out of that house."

When Nina was a child, there had been an autistic polar bear in the Bronx Zoo that spent all day pacing the length of his cage. Nina had always been upset but also intrigued by the misfit bear. Now Jonathan reminded her of the animal, a slightly maladjusted cold-weather mammal trapped in the tropics. She could empathize. He was wearing more clothes than ever. To his regulation cotton shirt and pants he had added shoes, socks, and a baseball cap. Chicago Cubs, no less. It was like wearing a button that said "I Am an Underdog." He didn't really need a button.

"Was it just Cheryl that drove you out of the house last summer?"

"No," he admitted. "There was a wide variety of factors."

"Such as?" She tried to sound concerned instead of nosy.

"Guess."

"Barry Adelman?"

"How did you guess?"

"Well, it sounds to me like you had a somewhat complicated relationship with him."

"Like you do with Cheryl."

"Something like that."

"Look, I don't really want to discuss Barry." Here it comes, she thought. Nina got ready to listen to him switch the conversation to the National League baseball standings. But he stayed on the topic. "I'm really blown away by his death. Despite the complications of our relationship, he was my oldest friend. And I feel like a piece of me is gone." It was trite, but Jonathan sounded convincing.

"Okay, we don't have to talk about Barry. Who do you want to talk about?"

"We could talk about Cheryl some more." Jonathan was being a good sport.

"Why don't we talk about you?" She was genuinely interested. Right up there with gossiping was listening to the story of someone's life for the first time. She loved hearing people talk about themselves, their favorite topic. The only problem was that most tended to get repetitive. But the first time out was usually a pleasure. "Let's sit down." She gestured to a nearby bench.

Nina was aware that she looked better standing up than sitting down, especially in boxer shorts. She remembered the precise moment when she first noticed that her thighs had begun to spread. It had been at a young and tender age and she had never really gotten over the shock.

Thighs like hers were a burden, but there were beneficial consequences also. For she was sure that if all her body parts had been thin, and she had never felt the need to prevent someone's gaze from drifting downward, she never would have developed the conversational agility she had. And where would she be in Housing Court without it?

She let Jonathan sit down first and then turned on her conversational brights before he had a chance to shift his focus. Jesus, things were easier in the city where you didn't have to run around half naked. "You said yesterday that you grew up in a big old house in Douglaston Manor," she said, as she perched on the edge of the bench, thereby minimizing her thigh spread. "I don't really know anything about the neighborhood. What was it like?"

CHAPTER 14

"**Douglaston Manor is a very old neighborhood.**" Jonathan sat back on the bench. He didn't have to worry about thigh spread. "It dates back to colonial times, actually. It's bordered by Nassau County on one side and Little Neck Bay on the other. And the rest of Queens to the south. Which, of course, everyone prefers to ignore. They'd rather look to the east and the north."

"You mean that they think of themselves as a western extension of Great Neck?" Nina had recently had the occasion to spend some time in Great Neck and she still hadn't gotten over it.

"No. Great Neck is too nouveau riche. In Douglaston Manor, it's more like they think of themselves as a southern extension of Beacon Hill."

"No Jews?"

"There are Jews everywhere now. Even in Beacon Hill.

And certainly in Douglaston Manor. As a matter of fact, I happen to be a Jew."

"You are?" Nina wasn't really that shocked. This had happened to her before. But the ones that she misdiagnosed always had some story—sent to boarding school or raised by a Christian aunt or something. They weren't Jews the way she was a Jew—a really big Jew.

"I am, although there's been some intermarriage in my family." Intermarriage in previous generations was typically an indication of wealth. Choosing a Christian spouse was something that never occurred to Nina's hardworking ancestors, who had considered a match between a Litvak and a Galiciana to be controversial. It was as if the rich could afford to shop anywhere, while the schleppers took whatever was at the corner store.

All that had changed, of course. Now almost anyone who had gone out of town to college had at least one interfaith fling in their past, if not a lawful union.

"Intermarriage on both sides," he continued. "But I consider myself Jewish."

"I guess it's dominant," she said. "Like brown eyes." Nina didn't really believe that. Her private theory was that if your maternal grandmother was a Jew, that pretty much shaped you. The Jews knew what they were doing when they determined the religion to be inherited matrilineally. A Jewish father could fade into nothing more than a piece of exotica, like having a pronounced widow's peak or an unusual hair color. But a Jewish mother locked you into the faith.

"Maybe. Anyway, when I was growing up, the neighborhood was still pretty Waspy. We had a large Tudor with a rose garden, a wood-paneled station wagon, an English sheepdog, and we kept a sailboat in the Sound."

"It sounds more like living in Marblehead than Queens."

"We never spoke the word *Queens*. I went to a private academy in Sands Point up until high school."

"How come your parents sent you to public school in the middle of everything?"

"It's hard to say. They went on some kind of egalitarian kick, making a big deal about how they didn't want me turning into a snob. But it's always been my opinion that the move was financially motivated. My grandmother died around then and I got the impression that her will said something different from what my parents were expecting. So they went on a big economy drive. They even discussed selling our summer house in Chester."

Nina had heard of Westchester and Eastchester but never of Chester. "Where's that?"

"Nova Scotia."

"Kind of tough to get up there for weekends, isn't it? I mean, it's not exactly the Catskills."

"We always spent August there. My parents still do. My mother flies up and opens the place while my father sails our boat up."

"Would you like to change lives with me?" It certainly sounded better than her childhood summers at Camp Wel-Met and her aggravating weekends in Westhampton Beach.

"It has its good and bad points. Chester is amazingly beautiful. All the charm of a small fishing village polished to a dazzling sheen with wealth. Picturesque without any dirt."

"What are the bad points?"

"My father. Also my mother."

"No siblings?"

Jonathan shook his head. "Only child."

"How classy."

"It's a real burden, believe me."

"Siblings have their good and bad points. What's wrong with your parents?"

"My father's your classic controlling bastard. And my mother . . . I don't know. She tries so hard to pass herself off as a rich WASP, but she gets it all wrong. As if she studied only their bad points. She trained herself to be cold and critical, although I still believe that underneath there's a real person. She's a mix. Picture the mother in *Ordinary People* being played by Julie Kavner instead of Mary Tyler Moore."

Nina was fascinated. She loved it when someone's life story had dramatic potential, when it was larger than life. This was probably a reaction to her bored childhood, when everything seemed smaller than life. "So, do you maintain cordial relations with them?" she asked.

"Off and on. We didn't speak for a couple of years after my marriage."

His marriage. Shit, was it possible that she'd misinterpreted his availability? "Oh," she said dully. Nina forced herself to maintain eye contact, but it was hard. The urge to sneak a look at his ring finger was almost irresistible.

"Actually, the not speaking lasted longer than the marriage," he said.

Thank you, God. "How long was that?"

"I was only married for about a year and a half. Ages ago. It was a ridiculous match, just a postadolescent rebellion on my part. She was a bad girl. At the time, I liked that. I guess you could say I was sexually addicted to her."

"How did you get yourself to leave?"

"She left me. She moved in with this actor. A very blue-collar guy, Italian and gorgeous, who had just landed his first big role."

"Anybody I would have heard of?"

"I don't think so. He had a short career. I think he ended up a junkie."

"What happened to her?"

"Oh, she landed on her feet. Married someone old and

rich who looked like a frog. They had a couple of little girls who unfortunately inherited his face."

"And your parents weren't good sports about all this?"

"Hardly. My father said she was just after my money. Of which, he pointed out, I didn't have any. And he intended to keep it that way. My mother was very upset about the fact that I was marrying a Catholic."

"But I thought you said that they were used to intermarriage in your family."

"I had one of those Jewish mothers that want you to marry a Protestant."

"Did they come to the wedding?" Nina asked.

"No. We just went to city hall and then had a big party in a friend's apartment. I knew they wouldn't come. I was so furious that when we moved and got a new phone number, I kept it unlisted and never gave it to them."

"Well, it seems that they were right about her."

"Yeah, but the funny thing is that I'd do it again. I was the happiest I'd ever been. I was on a continual sexual high. And if I had a sneaking suspicion that she was cheating on me from time to time, it didn't seem to matter all that much."

A thought occurred to Nina. She wrestled with the impulse to voice it. It was a no-contest wrestling match, however. It always was. Once she got the urge to blurt something out, she was almost powerless to keep her mouth shut. "What did Barry think of her?"

"He thought she was hot." Jonathan looked visibly upset.

Nina decided to drop the subject. The point had been made. "How did you reconcile with your parents?" she asked.

"It was a couple of months after my wife had moved in with Joey. A cousin of mine was getting married. I knew that my parents would be there and I dreaded the inevitable barrage of *I told you so*s. But I was pretty close to this cousin and I decided to go anyway. As soon as I got there, my mother broke into tears and threw her arms around me."

"That doesn't sound very much like the mother in *Ordinary People*."

"I told you. As played by Julie Kavner."

"So it was all fine from there on in?"

"I wouldn't say it was exactly fine. There was the time I invited them over for dinner and left a copy of *Toxic Parents* on the coffee table."

"They must have loved that."

"I'll admit it was provocative. Basically, we've gone back to the ambivalent, tortured parent-son relationship that we always had. Which we've managed to maintain without major conflagration for another two decades."

Nina was usually turned on by the use of *ambivalent* in a sentence. It showed that the speaker had probably been in therapy. Which, on the Upper West Side, Nina's home turf, meant you spoke the same language. But out here, in the Land of the Id, the term seemed a little out of place. Like Jonathan himself. What was he doing out here anyway? She decided to explore this angle. "How long have you been coming out here?" she asked.

"This is my second summer."

"Do you like it?"

"To tell the truth, after last season I didn't think I'd come back. Although I got along with most of the people in your house. Harriet's nice, and I got pretty friendly with Charlie and Ira. The rest of them can be amusing. But Cheryl gave me a headache. And it was ridiculous to think that Barry and I could coexist under one roof. I considered forgetting the whole thing and renting out in the Hamptons. But the thought of all those traffic jams and tennis games wasn't very appealing. So I decided to try another house."

"Is that working out better?"

"Much. I'm glad I did it. Davis Park really is a magical place. It's more than just relaxing. It's transcendental."

"There's a word you don't hear much anymore."

"But it's true. You can feel like an entirely different person out here," he said. "Totally carefree."

"When there's no one getting murdered, that is."

"Right." Jonathan sat silently for a few moments. "Want to take a walk on the nature trail?" It was the Watch Hill way of asking someone to come up and see your etchings.

"Sure," she said, without a second thought.

CHAPTER 15

"Where have you been?" Cheryl asked, the minute Nina walked into the house. She was seated in a chair by the door, as if lying in wait.

"I went for a walk." Nina sat down next to her. "Where is everybody?"

"Around. A couple of them went next door. Where did you walk to?"

"Out east."

"How far?"

"Just to Watch Hill."

"You were gone an awfully long time." Cheryl was in a relentless mood. For a change.

"I ran into someone." Nina knew she would end up telling Cheryl everything, but she didn't want to rush things.

"Anyone I know?"

"Yes."

"And who might that be?"

Nina gave a sigh of surrender. "Jonathan."

"Awright!" Cheryl sounded wildly enthusiastic. Why did she care so much? She had never seemed like the type who had matchmaking urges. If anything, she was a sexual cynic, who talked about men the way Ralph Nader used to talk about General Motors.

"And?" Cheryl persisted.

"And what?"

"Where did you go?"

"Go? This is Fire Island. There's no place to go."

"So what did you do?"

"There's nothing to do."

"Come on." Cheryl sounded genuinely annoyed.

"I'm only quoting you," Nina said. She let Cheryl build up a little more steam. "Okay, okay," she said, giving in. "We went for a walk on the nature trail."

Cheryl gave her a lascivious look. "Take a walk on the nature trail," she sang, to the tune of that old Lou Reed song "Walk on the Wild Side."

"Oh, come on, it was completely innocent."

"So why are you blushing?"

Nina *was* blushing. It was at times like these that she cursed her fair coloring. "Well, almost completely innocent. This is really none of your business."

"What does that have to do with anything?" Cheryl glared her into submission. It wasn't that hard. Nina was sure that Cheryl had worthier opponents. Like Barbara. She'd like to see those two go at it.

"Okay, nothing much happened. He kissed me once, that's all. At the part where the trail empties out into the wetlands."

"Oh, yes. The wetlands. That'll do it every time. The wetlands are famous for that sort of thing."

"They are? I had no idea." It had been romantic—the

gulls and the marsh grasses and the boats in the distance. A perfect place to succumb.

"So what do you think?" Cheryl asked.

"Of the nature trail? I'd been there before. It's very nice."

"Don't be coy. I hate coy. What do you think of him?"

"I like him. I mean, he seems pretty neurotic, with all these parental issues. And even though we didn't discuss it, I'll bet he has a few career issues also. He's sort of a mess, I guess. But a nice mess."

"He's perfect for you." Cheryl gave a little laugh that could be considered insulting. But Nina knew Cheryl was right. Jonathan was perfect for her. And admitting that somehow made her nervous.

"I don't know. I wouldn't necessarily say perfect. Ballpark maybe."

"A very small ballpark. Smaller than Fenway, I'd say."

"Okay, let's just say that there's some potential there and leave it at that."

"So what are you going to do about all that potential?"

"I said some potential, not 'all that potential.' "

"What are you going to do about it?" The Red Queen had returned.

"Well . . . uh, I'll see. I'm going out on his boat tomorrow morning."

"Well, that's that. If you think the wetlands were hot, wait until you're out on his boat. You'll be absolutely powerless to resist his advances."

"I don't know if he's going to make any advances," Nina protested.

"He will. You'd better bring some protection. And I don't mean your tube of number fifteen."

"I'm not going to sleep with him."

"And why not?" Cheryl sounded like she was taking it personally.

"For one thing, I've got to take Tom into consideration."

"Are you crazy? You know that's a dead end."

"How come you're so sure?" Nina asked.

"First of all, you'll never get him out of that place he lives in, whatever it's called."

"Lake Placid."

"Whatever. And somehow I don't see you moving up there and working for Frozen Tundra Legal Services."

"I don't necessarily mean that I'm going to marry the man. But I do happen to be maintaining a sexual relationship with him at the moment."

"Is that what you're maintaining? Or are you maintaining a holding pattern so that you can avoid confronting the hard issues of commitment and marriage?"

This didn't sound like Cheryl. The whole conversation felt like Nina was having it with somebody else. "Look who's talking. I don't see you choosing your bed partners by their marriage potential. I mean, Barry Adelman wasn't exactly marching down any aisles."

"Barry was a mistake. But he was an easy mistake to make. You heard everyone. Even Harriet slept with him, for Chrissakes."

"Okay. But what makes you think that Jonathan is marriage material?" Nina asked.

"For one thing, he's been married before. And as all the magazine articles tell us, that's a good sign."

"I don't think that marriage really counts. He was very young and it was over practically before it started."

Cheryl leaned back in her chair and paused a few moments. "It might have worked if it wasn't for Barry."

"What do you mean? I thought the wife dumped Jonathan for a young Bobby De Niro type."

"That was only after her affair with Barry. When things were already going down the toilet."

"I did get the impression that there was some tension around this issue," Nina said.

"Tension? I'll say. Jonathan and Barry didn't speak for ages after that."

"Hmmm." Jonathan seemed to spend a lot of time not speaking to a lot of people. This was worrisome. Nina had never not spoken to anyone. It seemed an act of mad passion that she was incapable of committing.

"Jonathan still blames Barry for breaking up his marriage," Cheryl went on.

"Are you sure? He didn't say anything like that to me."

"I happen to know it for a fact. Actually, I'm surprised that Jonathan didn't kill him years ago."

"What's that supposed to mean?"

"I'm not really serious. But you never know."

"So why are you encouraging me to run around with someone who might be a murderer?"

"Nothing ventured, nothing gained."

"And exactly what do you think I have to gain here?" Nina asked.

"Well, you certainly have nothing to lose."

"Gee, thanks." What did she have to lose? Maybe Tom. But to be honest, she no longer harbored any real expectations for that relationship. Nina and Tom were too different.

She had always sought out men with qualities that she lacked. Men that were hard where she was soft, that knew how to do things that she didn't. She was a sucker for those out-of-town types who could start a fire and tinker with a car engine and remain silent effortlessly. A good part of the reason she stayed with Grant so long was that his silences were so graceful. Tom's silences were less graceful, but what he lacked in quality, he made up in quantity.

But there was no real meeting of the minds. She worried that her motivation was, if not self-loathing, then at least a mild self-contempt. Not that she could fool herself into thinking that by pure effort alone she could will her heart into loving a man who had grown up on her block. But perhaps choosing a small-town lawyer who thought of New York City as a place where evil dwelled in the hearts of men was going overboard. Besides, she was getting sick of Tom's antiurban diatribes. He was starting to sound like Spiro Agnew or Dan Quayle.

She had never really felt like they had achieved that state known as "being good together." And lately they had seemed to be getting worse together.

Jonathan was something in between. In no way did he remind her of the Bronx, with his boat shoes and long-sleeved shirts of purely natural fibers. Yet he had that neurotic New York City homeboy quality, chattily introspective and full of Jewish-mother jokes. Maybe he was a good compromise. Besides, she thought he was cute. And she was still pissed at Tom for dumping her to go canoeing with his daughter.

"Jonathan's a very interesting guy," Cheryl said. "Complex. I think you'd enjoy him." She sounded as if she were recommending a bottle of wine. "And if it does turn out that he killed Barry . . . well, it won't be the first time you've gotten involved with a murderer, will it?"

No, it wouldn't. There had been Patrick, who she had fallen for in a big way. Well, he hadn't been an actual murderer. More of a manslaughterer. Nevertheless, Nina had to admit that he had not been a good choice. None of her long string of choices could really qualify as good, she supposed.

She didn't seem to have the best judgment in these matters. Maybe she should hire a professional. Shrinks were supposed to be helpful, but hers was of limited utility when it came to advice for the lovelorn. Her therapist preferred discussing what went on back in the Bronx when Nina was four years old. Sometimes she wondered if her shrink was doing research for a documentary film about the Grand Concourse in the 1950s.

Society had a need for a new kind of consultant, someone who would meet with you after a first date and tell you what dangers lay ahead. Someone who had no vested interest, who wouldn't turn into a *shiddoch*-crazed yenta like Cheryl had suddenly become.

Barbara came into the house. "It's clearing up," she said.

"Good," said Cheryl. "Maybe tomorrow will be a good day for sailing. Nina has a boating appointment."

"Oh. With Jonathan?"

"Yup," Cheryl said enthusiastically. "What do you think? Aren't they a perfect match?"

"It depends." Barbara sounded cautious.

"On what?" Cheryl sounded like she was challenging her to a duel.

"On whether Nina can put up with a man who won't take his clothes off."

"Oh, stop," Cheryl said. "That's ridiculous."

"Have you ever seen him in a bathing suit?"

"Of course I have."

"Then what's the story? Does he have some horrible scar or leprosy or something?"

"Of course not."

"So why does he walk around with everything rolled down to his toes no matter how hot it is?" Barbara said. "I can't figure out how come he wears those shirts all the time. I'd be careful if I were you, Nina. He might just be looking for a woman who can pay his bills at the Chinese laundry. Which are pretty steep, I would imagine."

The two of them discussing Jonathan made Nina uncomfortable. She could see it now. She'd go out with him on his boat tomorrow, and by the following afternoon they'd be the primary topic of conversation in town. There was something sick about everybody knowing exactly what everyone else was doing all the time. She had a strong urge to go back to the city. It was true that back there you had to be sure to lock up your pocketbook. But at least you weren't constantly under the scrutiny of a battery of electron microscopes.

"I'm going for a walk," Nina said.

"You just went for a walk," Cheryl said.

"I'm going for another one." She was starting to feel like the autistic polar bear pacing in its cage.

CHAPTER 16

"**Boy, what you missed,**" said Cheryl, lying in wait again by the door when Nina returned from her second long walk of the day.

"What?"

"Late-breaking news," called Barbara from the kitchen. Dinner was apparently in the process of being prepared, since there were at least eight people stepping all over each other, washing lettuce, mincing garlic, chopping onions, and skewering marinated chunks of chicken.

Cheryl pulled Nina over to a corner of the living room. "Listen to this," she said.

"Wait a minute. Should I be helping in the kitchen?" Nina wasn't crazy about the thought of chopping onions. But whenever she found the task distasteful, she reminded herself of the months she'd spent working in a kibbutz kitchen. There onion chopping was one of the preferred assignments. The worst was fish preparation. The fish came whole and unscaled. The first thing you had to do was drop them in the electric potato-peeling machine to get the scales off. The next job was to cut off the tail and head, slit the belly, scoop out the guts, hose the thing down, pull out the major bones, and cut it into edible serving-size pieces. The kibbutz was a large one and a fish meal typically required the dismemberment of hundreds of specimens.

The second worst was beet night. Beets were dangerous things, a lethal combination of hard-to-remove grit and a color that was guaranteed to permanently ruin whatever you were wearing. Unfortunately, fresh beets were a great Israeli favorite and Nina returned to the United States with reddish purple stains all over her wardrobe.

So chopping a few onions seemed like no big deal. Besides, a good guest is a helpful guest. It said so on a sign over the kitchen sink, right next to the one that said "Clean up after yourself. Your mother is not here this weekend."

"I mean, everyone looks so industrious," Nina continued. "I don't want them to think I'm useless."

"Stay out of the kitchen," Cheryl warned. "It's a madhouse in there. I always find it preferable to clean up after dinner, when everyone's fled."

Nina agreed. There was something meditative and soothing about solitary dishwashing—while food preparation was inherently stressful, with deadlines and performance anxiety and a comment period. "Okay." Nina sat down on the couch. "What's the late-breaking news?"

"The autopsy's done. And it's true that Barry was poisoned. But you'll never believe by what." Cheryl paused for dramatic effect.

"Tell me." Nina indulged in a whine.

"A patch."

"What kind of patch? Like a berry patch?" Nina hadn't

seen any blueberries or wild raspberries growing around the island, but maybe she had missed something.

"No, you idiot. One of those patches that you put behind your ear to ward off motion sickness."

"You're kidding."

"Nope. Someone added poison to it before Barry attached it to his skin. And keep in mind that he was going sailing the next day. With Jonathan." Cheryl had lowered her voice. But she was hissing with such histrionic urgency that Barbara, who was on kabob duty at the kitchen counter, heard what she was saying.

"Sailing with Jonathan," Barbara repeated. "Isn't that what you're doing tomorrow, Nina? Hope you're not prone to getting seasick. Because I wouldn't go near any transdermal medication if I were you." The fishbowl syndrome was hitting early. Nina felt faint of heart. The phone rang. Nina was closest, so she picked it up. It was Jonathan.

"Hi," he said, managing to convey quite a bit of warmth with just one syllable. It reminded Nina that she was in the middle of something good happening to her.

"Hi." She tried to convey warmth back. So far it was one of the better phone conversations she'd had with a man in quite some time.

"Listen," he said. "About tomorrow. I know I said we'd go out on the boat but something's come up."

Bullshit. What could come up in Davis Park? "What's that?" She tried to sound decent, but it came out a little sharp.

"The police want me in for questioning. First thing tomorrow."

"Really?"

"I'm afraid so." He sounded oppressed. More so than usual. "Maybe we can go for a sail when I get back."

"That would be nice. I'll probably be around the house.

Just come over." The good thing about Fire Island was that you could tell someone to come over without specifying which meal you were going to feed them. And should the demand for a meal arise, Wheat Thins always seemed to constitute an adequate entree.

"Great. I'll see you tomorrow. Take care."

"You too." It had been the first phone call Nina had received at the house. Barbara and Cheryl had been listening in, along with the rest of the kitchen patrol.

"Are you having company?" Cheryl asked.

"Jonathan's been asked to talk to the police tomorrow morning. So I told him to come over when he was through."

Cheryl jumped right on top of that piece of information. "What do they want to talk to him about?"

"I didn't ask. I didn't want to pry."

"Since when?" Cheryl snapped. "Prying is usually one of your major activities. You're a world-class pryer."

"A good pryer is a selective pryer. I'll pry tomorrow," Nina promised. "That way I'll get the whole story."

Charlie came in from the deck. "The coals are ready. Should I put the chicken on the grill?" It was amazing that even in a world dominated by women and Jews, it was still the lone male Christian that tended the flames.

"Okay," said Nancy. "The salad's ready. Let's eat that while the kabobs cook."

"No," said Charlie. "Let's have the salad after the main course."

"Here comes our local nightly entertainment," Cheryl said. "Watching Charlie try to convince everyone to eat the salad course last. This went on all last summer and it continues. He never prevails, of course, but he keeps on trying."

"He didn't say anything last night," Nina said.

"Last night we had gazpacho instead of salad. And the night before we had steamed artichokes. We'll do anything to prevent Charlie from arguing about this. But sometimes you just have to have salad."

As a matter of fact, Nina had lived a life without salad for many years. She ate it, of course, if it came her way. But she never made an active attempt to procure it. She had experienced a late-adolescent onset of an aversion to cleaning lettuce. She hated all the dirt and the endless paper towels used in a futile attempt to dry off the leaves before they wilted. Nina had mostly avoided lettuce all through her twenties, sometimes resorting to a four-dollar head of hydroponic greens, which were clean as a whistle. When August came, she went for straight tomato salads, always explaining that there was some undesirable chemical reaction between tomatoes and other vegetables and that they should properly be eaten separately.

Years later, well into her thirties, she read a book by Julia Child titled *The Way to Cook*. According to Julia, the correct way to wash lettuce was to fill a very large bowl with very cold water, separate the leaves, throw them in one by one, and let them soak for a few minutes. Nina tried the method and found that the dirt fell right to the bottom. She scooped out the leaves and threw them into a salad spinner she had borrowed from a neighbor. She was free. Her salad phobia had reversed itself. She bought her own spinner and started taking joy in plunging the leaves into their icy bath and examining the dirty remains on the bottom of the bowl. She found herself speaking the words "I'll make a salad" with genuine enthusiasm.

"Why does Charlie want to eat the salad course last?" she asked.

"Because it's more French that way."

"And how come nobody else does?"

"Because," Cheryl said impatiently, "who the hell wants

to bother eating a bunch of raw vegetables when you're not even hungry anymore?"

"I see your point." But personally Nina found the idea appealing. She liked the sophistication of being in a house that ate its salad right before the cheese course. Of course, there were no cheese courses anymore, what with high-density lipids and all, but it sounded good. She pictured herself the following winter at a cocktail party. She'd be dressed in black (Nina often had fantasies of winter outfits during the times when she was forced to wear boxer shorts) and say casually, "Oh, I rented out on Fire Island last summer. We had such marvelous meals, hours and hours long. By the time we finished the salad course and were ready for dessert, it was usually elevenish."

But this was not to be. Because Elizabeth and Estelle quickly set the table while Nancy dressed the salad. Charlie insisted on saving his portion for later, while everyone else sat down and dug in. "Good salad, Nancy," Ira said. "What's the taste I don't recognize?"

"Probably cilantro. Maybe I put too much in."

"Oh, no. It's perfect." Nina loved cilantro. Its flavor was elusive. She could never remember what it tasted like when she wasn't eating it. But her first bite always brought back joyful memories.

"So what are the police questioning Jonathan about?" Maggie asked. "That fight he had with Barry last week?"

"That was a doozy," Cheryl said.

"Don't be ridiculous," Harriet said. "That wasn't a fight."

"What was it then?"

"That's the way people sound when they're talking about money."

"Why were they talking about money?" Nina asked.

"Oh, Barry and Jonathan were always talking about money," Harriet said. "Barry thought he could make Jonathan rich. He fancied himself some kind of lay investment counselor."

"Why Jonathan? Why didn't he try to make himself rich instead?"

"Because," said Cheryl, "Barry never had any capital of his own. Womanizing is expensive, you know."

"I don't like the way this sounds," said Nina. She hadn't realized that Barry and Jonathan had financial dealings. Which was one step away from being business partners. And, as everyone knew, business partners exhibited an occasional tendency to kill each other.

"They were legitimate deals," Maggie said. "Don't get us wrong. It wasn't like Barry was Jonathan's connection to Bogotá or anything like that."

"You look nervous," Harriet said. "You shouldn't worry about Jonathan. He's a doll."

"Appearances can be deceiving," Cheryl said.

"Men can be deceiving," Barbara added.

"So can women," Charlie said as he mournfully watched everyone finish their salad.

CHAPTER 17

Nina had to wait for the second pot of coffee the following morning. It was in the morning, when everyone had coffee and bathroom requirements, that the house felt the most crowded. Today was Monday. Nina thought that some of them would have left already. She asked Cheryl about it without trying to appear rude.

"How come no one left last night?" she said, once they were settled on the deck. "I thought Sunday evening was exodus time. Not that I mind, of course. I'm enjoying everyone's company."

"Like hell you are."

"No, really. I am."

"Wait until you can't get to the toilet when you need it. Then you'll see how much you enjoy everyone's company."

The thought worried Nina. Constipation was a bad childhood memory, something she had beaten back. But she

couldn't lick the feeling that all it would take was one occu-
pied bathroom to knock her out of remission.

"The reason that everyone's still here," Cheryl said, "is
that we had a sort of house meeting. At first everyone was
ready to get on the next ferry. I mean, a murder isn't something that makes you want to hang around indefinitely. But
we all finally agreed that we would stay a week to see what
happened. To give each other moral support."

Nina didn't get it. "But no one seems particularly broken
up about Barry's death." It was amazing, really. Business as
usual. There had been one brief discussion about who was
going to order the next week's groceries now that Barry
wasn't around. But except for Jonathan's initial reaction,
there had hardly been a tear shed. Even Harriet, with her
acute case of niceness, was practically sailing through the
postmortem.

"Well, it's upsetting, of course, to find a dead body in the
upstairs bedroom. But are any of us really mourning him?
Probably not."

"How come?" Nina asked. "You were all pretty intimate,
I'd say."

"Precisely. Too intimate. I think that if a man is your
lover and then stops being your lover, then it's almost like
he's dead to you. And all the women in the house were in that
situation. You heard us. So it's as if we've all already mourned
Barry's death when we stopped sleeping with him."

"An interesting theory. Except that I'm not so sure all
those women were finished with him." Nina had gotten the
impression that at least some were still willing to sneak off for
a quickie from time to time.

"You may be right. But Mindy had gone after him in a
big way. She was already talking rings. All based, of course,
on her fantasies. But Barry went pretty public with their rela-

tionship. Mindy was no backdoor woman. And the rest of the house sort of dropped back. So in a sense it was over for us."

"And when Mindy stormed out of the picture?"

"Barry was all involved with Angela by then. And the truth is, we were all a little intimidated by Angela."

"She looked a little scary." Nina had a vague recollection from Friday night of a woman with bristling black hair and eyes. "Do you think she killed him?"

Cheryl narrowed her eyes and stretched in a very feline manner. "No," she said simply.

"Why not? She looked to me like someone who—"

"No." Cheryl repeated, cutting Nina off. "She's not a likely suspect."

"Okay. How about Ira and Charlie? They never slept with Barry, did they?"

"Of course not."

"Well, I couldn't be sure. After all, Estelle said the man would fuck a knothole in a pine board, didn't she?"

"Barry didn't have time to chase after same-sex partners. He was busy enough."

"So how come Ira and Charlie aren't in mourning?" Nina asked.

"They probably wished he was dead a long time ago."

"How come?"

"Ira and Charlie are great guys. But they have no luck with women."

"Why not? Market conditions couldn't be better."

"They aim too high," Cheryl explained. "Either one of them could have been happily married years ago to someone like Harriet. But nooo. They're always running after women that look like Jenny. Remember Jenny?"

"Yeah." Nina recalled mostly the waist-length strawberry-blond hair, but she got the idea.

"I think they became fixated on that type during their freshmen year of college and got stuck there."

"So they were jealous of Barry? Or is that an oversimplification?"

"It might be a simplification, but it's not an oversimplification. Basically, yes, Ira and Charlie were jealous of Barry."

Jealousy. Nina was never comfortable using the word. But the emotion existed. She found that if she swallowed her jealousy with a side shot of condescension, it went down better. So she was always reminding herself that her sister was really only a glorified housewife. "Jealous enough to kill him?" Nina asked.

"What do you think?"

Nina couldn't picture it. "Nah."

" 'Nah' is right."

"Anyway, getting back to the original topic, what kind of moral support is everyone hanging around to give? I don't understand what you mean."

"Well," said Cheryl, "the police have questioned everyone in the house."

"I know. But are any of you suspects?"

"I can't say for sure. But some of their questions have been very unnerving."

"Like what?"

"I don't really want to go into it now," Cheryl said. "But they're using divide-and-conquer tactics, arousing suspicions and trying to cause splits. So we got together and discussed it and decided that if we all stayed out here for a while, it would provide better damage control. Besides, it's a holiday week and most of us were planning on being out anyway."

"But what if one of you is guilty? Why are you so concerned with damage control? Isn't it more important to find out the truth? I mean, house solidarity is very nice as a concept. But do you really want to be sharing living quarters with a murderer?"

"I don't think anyone in the house did it. None of us does. Otherwise we wouldn't be protecting one another."

"So who do you suspect?" Nina asked. Cheryl didn't answer.

"Good morning." The voice came from the boardwalk. It belonged to Jonathan.

"Look who's here. That was fast," Cheryl said. "Have they put you on the Ten Most Wanted list yet?"

"It's possible." Jonathan sat down in the deck chair next to Nina. "They told me not to go anywhere for a while."

"Really?" Cheryl seemed most interested.

"Yeah, which is a problem. Because I've got to get the boat back to my father in about a week."

"I thought you said he only used it in August," Nina said.

"It takes two weeks to get it up to Nova Scotia. Sailboats only go seven miles an hour, you know."

"So he spends as much time taking it there and back as he does having it there."

"Before he retired, he used to hire someone to sail it there and back. Now he does it himself."

"It hardly seems worth it," Nina said. She wondered whether she had the patience to enjoy moving at seven miles an hour. She couldn't even get herself to take the Fifth Avenue bus. She'd rather walk all the way over to Lexington and jump on the IRT. She knew her attitude was narrow, that the sheer joy of performing the act made it worthwhile. And a scenic view of Fifth Avenue was something to enjoy. But it was difficult to experience joy while you were looking at your watch. And Nina, over the years, had become quite a watch watcher. Maybe she should go back to smoking marijuana.

Hers was the prevailing attitude of the lower middle class, one that she couldn't shake no matter how many Mount Hol-

yoke grads she hung around with. She could never understand how someone could have the patience to grow orchids
or bake their own pastries. Patience was a province of the
privileged.

"Oh, it's worth it," Jonathan said. "There's nothing like
sailing."

"Why doesn't he just leave it up there?"

"And miss June and half of July and September? What a
waste. September's the best, if you ask me."

"I'll bet." Nina tended to agree. She always looked forward to that time of the year when she could put away her
boxer shorts.

"So why do the police want you to hang around?" Cheryl
asked.

"They think I make a good suspect. After all, Barry was
poisoned by a patch he put on because he was supposed to be
going sailing with me."

"Do they know who gave him the patch?" Cheryl asked.

"I don't know."

"Who do you think gave it to him?"

"I don't know."

"Come on, Jonathan," Cheryl said. "Cut the 'I don't
know' crap. Surely you have some theories about who murdered Barry."

"I'd hate to think it was anyone I knew. Maybe it was that
kid he was running around with at Sunmist on Friday night.
She was the last one seen with him."

"Kim?"

"Is that her name?"

"I believe so." Cheryl waited until the silence got uncomfortable. "It's a nice theory, Jonathan, but quite frankly, she
didn't look much like a murderer to me."

"Well, who do you think did it?" he asked Cheryl.

"I have my theories. But they're not to be shared with the general public."

Nina couldn't stand listening to the conversation anymore. It was bound to turn nastier. "Are we going sailing or what?" she said.

"Sounds good to me."

"Make sure you bring him back, Nina. After all, the police don't want him to stray too far."

"Don't worry. We'll be back in time for dinner," Jonathan said. He was being a good sport. Cheryl was really asking for it. Someone should have boxed her about the ears. But it wasn't going to be Nina, that was for sure.

"Have a good time, you two," Cheryl said, sounding for all the world like Margaret Hamilton in *The Wizard of Oz.*

CHAPTER 18

The boat looked exactly the way a sailboat was supposed to look, kind of old and weathered, with a lot of wood. It probably wasn't the swiftest craft in the water, but it had all the proper connotations of old money. It stood out among the stinkpots that crowded the Davis Park marina. The motorboats were fiberglass, with no more than a few inches of token wood trim. Jonathan's sailboat was straddled by two cabin cruisers, one named *Donna Marie II* and the other named *Gelt*. They were both chunky and loaded down with beach chairs and grills and beer-filled coolers. They made the sailboat look especially delicate and fine-boned.

His boat was named *Millicent*, after an aunt whose inheritance had made its purchase possible. Nina tried to imagine having an Aunt Millicent, but it was a stretch. She did have an Aunt Malka, but she had become Molly. Nina was sure renaming herself Millicent had never occurred to her. Uh-oh, she felt herself slipping into a full-tilt Bronx boogie. She tried to rein herself in. She had been admitted to practice law, she reminded herself. Her post office was the Ansonia Station, one she shared with Mia Farrow and Kathleen Turner. She had a subscription to the New York City Ballet. She had roomed with a Presbyterian from Connecticut and a Baptist from North Carolina and had spent five years sleeping with a Lutheran from Wisconsin. In fact, she was sleeping with a Methodist from upstate New York at this very moment. Well, not technically at this very moment, but they were still officially an item.

Besides, Jonathan wasn't exactly a WASP. Maybe an Aunt Millicent and a woody sailboat was enough to pass as far as Nina was concerned. But she knew that there were still plenty of country clubs that he'd have a hard time getting into. All right, she told herself. Forget the ethnic thing. There's still the class thing. Funny, class issues never seemed important when she was younger. But lately . . . well, it was as if you spent the first half of your life worrying about not being thin enough and the second half worrying about not being rich enough.

"What a beautiful boat," she said. If she kept talking, maybe she'd feel better. But she had a hard time thinking of what to say next. Sailboats were not something she knew anything about. Except that people like her didn't own them. And that was a topic she was trying to stay away from.

"I know. I love it. It's the sibling I never had."

"Oh, did you grow up with it?"

"It's not that old. It's a 1971 Hinckley B-40."

"Does that mean it's forty feet long?"

"Very good."

Her mood brightened as they got into the boat. Maybe she had some aptitude for this sort of thing after all. "Not great sailing weather, is it?" she asked. It had, for a change, clouded over.

"I like a little mist. It's more of a challenge. Sailing in the Great South Bay is pretty pointless. Weather gives you something to think about."

"Why is it pointless?"

"There's nowhere really to go, for one thing. You just sort of sail back and forth aimlessly."

"Oh." She couldn't help but think of the autistic polar bear, this time in a 1971 Hinckley B-40.

"In the Sound, at least you can go up to Block Island or Shelter Island or head up to New England. But here, the best you can do in a day is Westhampton Beach, and who wants to go there?"

"Not me." Maybe after Sandy Slotnick leaves, she thought. She pictured sailing out to her sister's and having Ken make a big deal about the boat. She supposed it could be gratifying on some level. But complicated on too many others. "So if it's pointless, why do you bother bringing the boat out here?"

Jonathan was quiet for a minute. "You know," he finally said, "I never really considered taking it out here until Barry got on my case about it. He thought it was a great idea."

"But you were less than enthusiastic?"

"Yeah. Help me unfold the sail, would you?"

"That sounds like something I could manage," she said. Unfolding was easier than folding. The act did not reveal her low standards when it came to that sort of thing. Her tendency was to wear poorly ironed shirts and to make a bed in a half-assed way so that you could swear that a couple of teenagers had just had wild sex in it.

She watched him raise the sail. He was casual in his movements, as if he'd been doing this from toddlerhood. "So why was Barry so hot on having the boat out here?" she asked.

"Why do you think?"

"Something to do with women?"

"You're a genius." He sat down next to her and playfully swatted her on the knee. She was immediately self-conscious. Her knee was far from her best feature. Now, if he had playfully shoved her shoulder or chucked her under the chin, it would have been vastly preferable.

"He thought that *Millicent* would help attract women?"

"Of course. As if he needed any help."

"Yeah," she said. "That guy had an amazing internal biochemical balance."

"Is that what it was? I always wondered."

"I think so. But then, I think everything is biochemical. It's my overreaction to being raised by parents who believed all traits to be environmentally determined. The word 'genetic' was not permitted to be spoken in our house."

"You can hardly blame them," he said. "I mean, which way would you come out on the controversy if Hitler was around, screaming all the time about the purity of the Aryan nation? They had no choice but to take a hard line."

She had never thought of that. "You've got a point. I guess I'd be a bit hypersensitive about biological predetermination under those circumstances. But the forbidden and illicit nature of genetics during my childhood made me fixate on it. Like Catholic school girls and sex."

"Only Jews believe that stuff about girls who went to Catholic school being hot. If you hang around with a bunch of Catholic guys, you'll see that they think the only ones who'll go down on you are Jewish girls."

It was a generous, if somewhat crude, statement. A regular Jewish guy would never say it. It was as if Jonathan's Christian blood made him more capable of appreciating his Jewishness. Instead of being overwhelmed and terrified by the unrelenting state of being a Jew, he had enough distance to get a kick out of it.

"Well, you know us. We'll put anything in our mouths." She would have felt more comfortable saying it if she had been dressed in control-top pantyhose and a long, full skirt instead of boxer shorts. But it was out before she could stop herself.

"Oh, please," he said. "You Jewish women and your weight. I could care less." Maybe he was lying. But just the fact that he said it was enough of a reason to follow him to the ends of the earth.

"Good" was all Nina said. She leaned back against the side of the boat and sat quietly, watching him steer them out into the bay.

"So you think that Barry's appeal was something he was born with, not learned behavior?" Jonathan asked.

"Why are you so concerned? Thinking of taking a course?"

"Do I need one?"

"I don't think so. But as it turns out, he's not really someone you'd want to emulate, is he?"

"No, but if you had asked me that question four days ago, you'd have gotten a different answer," he said.

"Did they give you a very hard time this morning? The police, I mean."

"Well, you see, I'm not in a great position. Do you know how he was poisoned?"

"I heard. With a motion-sickness patch, right?"

"Yeah. And if Barry wasn't going sailing with me that day, he wouldn't have put it on. And he wouldn't be dead."

"That doesn't mean anything. Did you know that he used those patches?"

"I did."

"And how many other people knew? Because everyone in my house seemed at least to know that the two of you were going on the boat the next day."

"I don't know who knew about the patches. The police asked me the same thing, of course. But I really couldn't give them an answer. He could have told everyone, or he could have told no one. I have no way of knowing."

"I guess it depends on whether he considered it a sign of weakness."

"Barry wasn't macho in the traditional sense," Jonathan said. "And you have to keep in mind that living in that house with eleven people, everyone seems to know everything."

"Right. The fishbowl syndrome."

"And he was very enthusiastic about the patches. He used them all the time, even if we were only going out for an hour. He thought they were the greatest invention."

Nina started to feel like she could use one herself. The wind was picking up and the bay was getting choppy. "Look," she said, "I don't see why the fact that you were taking him sailing makes you a suspect. It's not like you handed him a toxic patch to stick on behind his ear."

"No, but I . . ." Instead of finishing his sentence, Jonathan turned his attention to something that Nina was pretty sure was the boom. It looked like it could hit you on the head if you weren't careful. She wondered if that was why they called it the boom.

"But you what?" she asked. "What did you do?"

"Nothing."

"What were you going to say?"

He just shrugged. Leave him alone, she told herself. Stop acting like a dog with a bone. You found a guy that thinks Jewish women are good in bed and doesn't care about their weight. Why start now with the Portnoy's mother routine?

"I'm sorry. Never mind. I didn't mean to cross-examine you."

But it was too late. Jonathan definitely looked put out. She considered offering to give him a blow job to compensate for her rudeness and to remind him of some of the good things about Jewish women. But a sailboat on choppy waters was probably a bad place to perform oral sex. Unless you were wearing a motion-sickness patch. And even though she was sure Jonathan was innocent of Barry's murder, she was not about to ask him if he had one on him.

CHAPTER 19

The rain came out of nowhere. No warning, no thunder, no lightning. A sudden thickening of the air and they were drenched. Jonathan sent Nina down into the cabin while he guided the boat back toward the marina.

The cabin was pleasant, wood paneled and cheery, and not at all claustrophobic. It was bigger than the bedroom that Nina and Cheryl shared in Davis Park. There was even a television, which she suspected got better reception than hers did in the city. She considered turning it on, but picked up a copy of *Yachting Magazine* instead. It was odd, she thought as she flipped past photos of boats that made this one look like a dinghy, how much rain they'd been having since she got out here.

The weather had changed about an hour after they found Barry's body and had never really cleared up. It had been wet on and off ever since. As if Fire Island had gone into permanent mourning for one of its prominent residents.

That was silly—she was sure it was also raining in Patchogue and Westhampton Beach and probably even on Broadway and Seventy-second. But things were definitely gloomy out here. She wondered if there would be a funeral. She hadn't heard anything.

Strange how the week was turning out. She remembered her fears as she waited for the ferry on Friday in the blazing sun. She had worried about the heat and the drinking and everybody else being tan and thin and sleeping with each other. But Barry's death had put a damper on all that. Everyone was still tanner and thinner than she was, of course. But it didn't show as much now that the sun had gone in. And Cheryl had barely gone near the blender in the past few days. As if the concept of a piña colada, Barry's favorite drink, had been retired right along with him. And as far as everyone sleeping with each other . . . well, it was as if the concept of sex, Barry's favorite activity, had been retired right along with him as well.

Instead she was stuck in a house filled with depressed people, waiting out the rain, alternating between watching videos and playing Trivial Pursuit. Which was really more up her alley than sun and fun.

And then there was Jonathan. Why was she so unsure about him? He looked pretty good, tall with lots of fluffy blond hair that fell into soft curls. A sweet face, almost pretty, and a body that looked sturdy enough, even if it did have a bit of extra padding. So why was she finding herself having to fight reluctance?

Maybe he wasn't her type. But Nina had always been wildly unsure of what her type really was. She had it figured out back during the Mick Jagger years, when she was attracted to anyone painfully thin and painfully androgynous. But this had turned out to be just an adolescent phase. Because later on she started to notice and appreciate various upper body muscle groups. And the men she'd gotten involved with over the years had been all over the map—tall and craggy, short and thick, pale and balding and laconic, dark and bristling with hair and energy. No clear pattern emerged.

Besides, Jonathan didn't really look like a type. He looked . . . well, the truth was he looked like Nina. Too many clothes, too much hair, too much flesh. They were the same type. Did that mean he was her type? It was hard to tell.

As she sat snuggled in the cabin's most comfortable chair, she tried to puzzle it out. Something was holding her back and she didn't know what it was. She wished she were one of those people who could just trust their instincts. But her instincts often proved as trustworthy as wet tissue paper. She'd have to figure it out cerebrally. The way she did everything.

Why did she always have to rely on her brain? It was tedious. Maybe it was like being blind. Blind people always developed superb senses of smell, hearing, and taste to compensate for their loss of vision. Maybe the only reason Nina was smart was because she had been born without instincts. And her mental powers had only developed to make up for her stumbling instinctual deficiencies.

She closed her eyes, breathed in and out deeply and slowly, and tried to summon up some instincts. She heard the voice of her aerobics teacher during the cool-down period telling her to relax into a stretch and get in touch with her inner self. But she drew a blank. It was clear that Nina had been born without a sixth sense. And the way things were going, she was lucky if she managed to hold on to the five she did have.

Because Jonathan made her feel out of control, more than she could remember feeling with any other man. Which was odd because he was quite gentle. She had certainly gone out with scarier specimens. But it seemed so easy just to take

Jonathan's hand and walk off into eternity. And that was really scary. Because even though she hardly knew him, hadn't even slept with him yet, she knew enough to see all the problems and pitfalls clearly. She saw it all spread out before her—his problems with his parents, with his career, with his self-esteem. And she knew that her system would just absorb it all, soak it right up like a double-ply roll of paper towels. And not even recognize any of it as a foreign substance. She had no antibodies for this stuff, there was nothing alien about the terrain of Jonathan's neuroses.

She had always feared that it would happen this way. That was the downside of self-awareness. You could see it all coming, no surprises. She still held on to a faint prayer that she would instead meet someone perched high on a pinnacle to pull her right out of her valley of self-doubt. Preferably someone played by Kris Kristofferson. Although she'd settle for an Al Pacino type. (She was, after all, a New Yorker and had to be realistic. And she had never seen someone in the flesh who reminded her even vaguely of Kris Kristofferson, now that she thought about it.) But in her heart she knew her prayer would go unanswered.

Her internal struggle with the concept of the inevitable was interrupted by Jonathan's calling her up to the deck. He poked his head in to tell her that there was a break in the rain. He looked so cute with his wet blond curls plastered against his forehead. What had she been worrying about? The inevitable did have its appeal.

"I think we should go back," he said, once they were up on the deck. "It looks like the rain will probably start up again."

"But I was having such a good time down in the cabin. It's probably the first time I've been alone in a room since I got here. Would you consider renting it to me?"

"Listen, anytime you need some privacy, just let me

know. The television gets good reception and the bed's really comfortable."

She let the reference to the bed slide. She was actually quite shy unless she was drunk. Nina suspected that most people were. Which explained why even though alcohol sales were down, they weren't way down. "Okay," she said. "Thanks, that's nice of you."

Nice. It was the operative word. He was nice. Or at least he was being nice to her. The term was no longer generally included in the postmodern dating vocabulary. There was *defensive* and *controlling* and *expansive* and *sensitive,* but *nice* had been banished. In fact, it was getting hard even to pronounce the word without giving it a nasty, cynical edge. Or a simpering, decayed sweetness that mocked the concept.

Of course, Nina knew that nice was an oversimplification. Jonathan could be nice and also be defensive and controlling and expansive and sensitive all at the same time. But he was being nice to her. She tried to distill the concept, to examine its essence, to separate it from any implications and complications. To not think about why he was being nice, what deficiencies that indicated, what sort of subtle form of manipulation he was trying to perform. But it was hard.

Coupling at this age was hard. Nina pictured a fresh-faced, virginal, small-town girl, late teens or early twenties, her eyes clear, her skin dewy, her ovaries pumping at maximum efficiency. The girl meets some young guy just hitting his testosteronal peak. They neck, set the date, and as soon as their barn is raised, they marry. That was the way the human race was meant to reproduce. Not like this, not sitting on a sailboat, perched on the edge of age forty, trying to figure out why he was being so nice to her.

Even so, she wasn't ready for retirement. That other favorite old-fashioned image, of the benevolent spinster, doing good works and helping rear other people's children, was as farfetched as the dewy virgin. Although she often felt as though she had excellent spinster potential. She had a career of her own, and as she got older, the idea of solitude had a more luxurious and less threatening cast to it.

Besides, she had been raised to stay outside of the mainstream, with a working, independent mother who tried hard to inject a healthy dose of bohemianism into her children. And the time and place were right. Manhattan was filled with intellectually dynamic people who lived alone and contemptuously referred to suburbanites as breeders.

But Nina also had a capacity for the mainstream. She was a straddler. She envied her sister, who had set off in one direction and never looked back—while Nina sat and watched her internal battle between the mainstream and the bohemian, back and forth as if at a tennis match.

Basically, she wanted to get married, even if only to move the plot along. She was getting tired of the same old issues. Besides, being married seemed so efficient. No more long trips to Lake Placid in fifteen-degree weather. And in one fell swoop, you halved your rent and utilities. And minimized your scheduling problems. Sometimes each weekend seemed like a jigsaw puzzle to Nina. It was a challenge to place all those brunches and movies and dinner parties in just the right position to pull off a successful weekend. Married people were exempt. When you asked them on Monday morning what they'd done, they just shrugged and said "nothing much" with a casual enthusiasm that Nina coveted.

Besides, she had always vowed to herself that she would do everything once. Unfortunately, this vow had been made during her undergraduate years of drug experimentation and had had some unpleasant results. But later she had moved on to foreign travel and other benign endeavors. Marriage was on her list, too—right below traveling to Portugal—

waiting to be crossed off. She had a strong suspicion that she'd probably get to Portugal first.

"So what are you doing Wednesday night?" Jonathan asked.

"Nothing much," she said, trying to infuse the words with casual enthusiasm.

"Want to do something?"

"Sure, we could do something."

"Good."

"Like what?"

"Something," he said.

"Okay, let's do something." She felt herself blushing. She noticed that he was too.

CHAPTER 20

It was on impulse, Nina knew, and she also had a strong feeling that she'd regret it. But it was Tuesday afternoon and the Slotnicks were probably safely headed west on the Long Island Expressway. Besides, Nina wasn't planning on spending any serious time out in Westhampton Beach. Just overnight, enough to get away from the tension of Barry's death and Jonathan's advances and Cheryl's personality.

Laura came to meet her at the station, which was a shock. Her sister had, apparently, finally overcome her decades of phobia and obtained a driver's license. That was something Nina was going to have to get used to. Now she'd have to find some other way, other than Laura's driving *mishegoss,* to comfort herself whenever she felt overwhelmed by feelings of inadequacy and sibling rivalry. The hard part was that Laura hadn't even seen fit to mention this, that she could be so casual about her ultimately triumphant wrestling match with her demons.

The other hard part was how good Laura looked. Despite a certain equine cast to her facial features, she was the kind of person who could, year after year, thank God that it was shorts season again. And order matching outfits for herself and Danielle from the Hanna Andersson catalog. If Nina was going to order a matching outfit with anyone, it was likely to be with her seventy-year-old mother and the catalog would have to be from one of those Kountry Klothes kind of places in the Berkshires that sold tunics and jumpers in tasteful floral prints.

Nina felt a little better watching Laura struggle with the Hamptons July traffic. Her sister drove like a thirty-six-year-old Jewish woman who had been raised in a borough and had just finally gotten her license. And Nina noticed that she was driving the Honda Prelude, not the Range Rover that Ken kept garaged out here, safe from the ravages of the city and his family. His wife might have her license, but her ability to operate a motor vehicle had its limits. Not that Nina blamed him, since Laura kept biting her lower lip and muttering and cursing, coming perilously close to all the upscale vehicles in which Dune Road specialized. Out here it was easy to pretend that you were in Southern California, the nadir of American civilization.

And while Davis Park had been spared the ravishes of nature over the past few years, Westhampton Beach had been hit hard. The way that Los Angeles now conjured up images these days of riots and earthquakes and mudslides instead of kumquats and grapefruits, parts of the Hamptons connoted disaster. Many of the large postmodern mansions had been left shakily on stilts, the rug pulled out from under them. Laura's house seemed untouched, the bay side having been less hard hit than the more expensive oceanfront property.

The house itself was charming, a gray shingled bungalow that had been standing since way before the Jews landed on the beachhead. Not that the Rubin family were pretenders to Waspdom. They were active members of the Garfield Temple and Nina had even witnessed her younger sister lighting *Shabbes* candles. Like many other young, affluent American families, they had embraced their ethnicity. The overassimilation issue that Philip Roth and Wendy Wasserstein struggled with on paper and stage seemed to be passé. Being a self-acknowledged Jew was hot these days. Especially if you were a man. *People* magazine was filled with photos of yarmulked studio executives and banking moguls rediscovering their roots. And some of their wives had even converted.

And there was her brother-in-law, watering some shrub in the driveway, wearing shorts and a polo shirt (with a capital *P),* looking as content as a clam at high tide. He was also wearing a pair of those new rubber all-terrain sandals, invented by a Colorado river guide and now worn even on Columbus Avenue. In case you should suddenly find yourself on tougher terrain than the West Seventies or Dune Road.

"Hey, Nina," he called. "How do you like my new clethra?"

Was that a bush or a sports car? It must have been a horticultural term, because all that was in the driveway was the same old Prelude and the Range Rover. Nina knew that whole chunks of life were passing her by, but it seemed psychotic to read the Smith and Hawkens catalog and *Road & Track* just to prepare herself for conversation on her occasional Hamptons weekend.

"It's beautiful, Ken. Sure it'll grow out here?" Everything on Dune Road looked so scrubby.

"The nurseryman said it would." He looked doubtful for a moment, as if his entire life's savings were tied up in this one investment. Nina knew that the life that her sister and brother-in-law had created only appeared low-maintenance. In order to pull it off, you really had to care about things.

About every single thing. A shrub required the same seriousness of attention as a child's ear infection or a life insurance policy.

Not that Nina didn't obsess about things. But she did it with the self-understanding of an acknowledged neurotic, with a sense of purposelessness that ultimately proved to be a relief, if not outright relaxing. She could drop it whenever she felt like it and pick it up again some other time. It was her hobby, something to do at an idle moment, like a half-finished sweater on knitting needles lying in a basket next to a hallway table.

Ken seemed to take his shrub more seriously than that, for he continued to mutter. "The thing cost enough. It had better do okay. There's no guarantee on plants, you know. It's not like a VCR that you can bring back before the warranty runs out."

"Where are the kids?" Nina asked.

"Inside," Ken said.

"He can't take his mind off his plants," Laura said, "to watch his children. Who's baby-sitting—Danielle?"

"She's good," Ken insisted. "The other day she changed Evan's diaper."

"She's not even eight years old," Laura said, "and you're using her for cheap labor."

"Yeah, I'm running a real slave camp here." Danielle and Jared had everything they could want, really. Attendance at the Berkeley-Carroll School and a summer day camp that specialized in marine biology. Even Evan, the baby, took an art class every Wednesday and got to go to Karatatot, a karate class for toddlers. Nina envied the children their lives, although she could do without the karate.

"They've been a little cooped up, with all this rain," Laura said. "Let's see what level of monstrosity they've descended to."

The sisters entered the house and were greeted by the sounds of a videotape at high volume. The kids watched a lot of television. All kids seemed to. Nina didn't really see it as evil. Playing your favorite videotape over and over seemed benign, like Woody Allen running off to see *The Sorrow and the Pity* whenever the opportunity arose. In fact, the world of videotapes seemed charmed to Nina. She remembered seeing Disney's *Alice in Wonderland* when she was small and waited years to see it again. The ability to own it, to watch it whenever you wanted . . . well, it made Nina think that she might have had, if not a happy childhood, then at least a less boring one.

"Okay, Aunt Nina's here," Laura shouted above the din. "How about we turn that thing off?"

Only the baby turned around. "Nina," he said, and toddled over to her. She picked him up and he pointed to the television screen. *"Pinocchio,"* he said.

"Yes, I see." *Pinocchio* was a sore point with her. The videotape had only been recently marketed for sale, billed as the last time that it would be available during this century. It made Nina feel as though she had missed some important childbearing deadline.

"Pinocchio," Evan repeated.

"Pinocchio," Nina agreed, and sat down with the kids to watch.

"Hi, Aunt Nina," Danielle said, and moved over into Nina's lap.

"Aunt Nina," Jared yelled into her ear, and draped himself over her shoulders.

"Hi, kids. How're you guys doing?"

"Okay," Danielle said.

"Evan called Daddy stupid," Jared said, again into her ear.

"Did he? That wasn't nice."

"Stupid," Evan cooed at Nina, as if paying her a compliment.

"I'm sure he meant it in the nicest way."

"He learned it from you," Danielle shouted at Jared.

"Did not."

Nina took this opportunity to remove Jared from her neck. "Sit down and be sweet and adorable, please," she said. "All of you. If I wanted to hear people snap at each other, I could have stayed on Fire Island."

"Fire Island?" Jared asked. "Was there a fire? Were there firemen?"

"No fire. No firemen. Hardly any men at all, as a matter of fact."

"Where did they go?"

"Good question. They all seemed to have disappeared a few years ago. Extinct, like dinosaurs."

"Oh." Jared looked troubled.

"She's just being funny," Danielle explained. "Aren't you?"

"Just you wait a few years. And see how funny it is to date a brontosaurus."

"Apatosaurus!" Danielle and Jared corrected her simultaneously.

"What?"

"They're not called brontosaurus anymore," Danielle said. "Now they're called apatosaurus."

Laura came in and sat down in a nearby chair. "What's she talking about?" Nina asked.

"They changed the name." Laura shrugged.

"Of a dinosaur? Something that's been extinct for millions of years? Why bother? It's not like we're talking about a car company that puts a new model on the market every year and has to appeal to consumer whims."

"Apparently brontosaurus wasn't correct enough. I don't know."

"What does that mean? Besides, who changed the name? Is there some Undersecretary of State for Extinct Reptiles, in Washington, that makes these decisions?"

"They're not sure they were reptiles, Aunt Nina," Danielle said. "Some scientists think that dinosaurs were warm-blooded."

"Is this true?"

"It's a theory," Laura said.

"Boy, am I out of it." Here was a previously unnoticed drawback to not having children. In addition to all the previously noticed drawbacks.

"What are you out of?" Ken had separated himself from his garden hose and come inside, bringing Nina's overnight bag with him.

"Nothing. Thanks," she said, and tossed the bag into a corner.

"Come into the kitchen," Laura said. "There's iced tea."

Uh-oh, Laura's dreaded iced tea. The Rubins were not a Snapple household. Laura steeped and brewed and squeezed all sorts of varieties of fresh produce to achieve her desired effect. Which always tasted somewhat medicinal to Nina.

"Okay." The adults drifted away from the sounds of *Pinocchio,* past the wall of glass blocks into the kitchen, a room that managed to be both homey and state-of-the-art.

"So what brings you out here?" Ken asked as Laura sorted through her collection of citrus squeezers.

"Murder and mayhem."

"Not again," Ken said. "You're getting to be a one-woman police blotter."

Somehow the phrase had unattractive overtones, like a human trampoline. "Wait until you hear about this one,"

Nina said. "It's right up your alley. As a dermatologist, I mean."

"What happened?"

"Laura didn't mention anything to you?"

"No."

"I told Sandy Slotnick about it," Laura offered, as if by way of explanation.

"Oh. Anyway, the reason I said it was right up your alley is because the poison was administered transdermally. In one of those seasickness patches."

"Clever," Ken said.

Laura handed them icy glasses of something the color of squid ink with sprigs of unidentified vegetation floating on top. Nina took a sip. It didn't taste much better than it looked. Or smelled. Sort of a cross between oolong and iodine. "Interesting," Nina said, using the universal donor of vocabulary words.

"It's my new house blend."

"Anyway," Nina continued, "this guy in my house, Barry Adelman, was supposed to be going sailing on Saturday. So on Friday night, he puts one of those patches on behind his ear."

"They take a few hours to kick in," Ken explained to Laura. "So if you're embarking early the next morning, you would probably put it on the night before."

"Right," Nina said. "He was embarking early on Saturday." She had never used the word "embarking" before. It was a classy word.

"When did someone tamper with the patch?"

"No one knows. Because he had the box of them for months. Someone brought them back from Canada for him."

"Yeah, they're over-the-counter there, aren't they?"

"How did you know?"

"I read the journals. They advertise heavily."

"Well, what do you think? Could it have been an accident? Could he have developed some sort of hypersensitivity or something?"

"That killed him? I doubt it. I thought you said that someone tampered with the patch."

"Rumor has it."

"What did they use? As a transdermal toxin, that is."

"I don't know. As I said, I've been relying solely on local gossip."

"Because there are many clever methods for killing someone transdermally, you know."

"Oh, really?" Laura said. "Given this some thought, have you?"

"Yes, as a matter of fact," Ken said. "There's a lot of literature on the subject. I've read about people getting murdered by someone tampering with their hand lotion, their aftershave, their suntan lotion, even their Retin-A. But this is the first I've heard of a motion-sickness patch being used as a weapon. I like it."

"And what kind of poisons did these murderers use?"

"Whatever was around. It's not hard. If they were gardeners, they might use some arsenic. If they're smokers, nicotine. Many poisons can be transmitted transdermally."

"Well, that doesn't help narrow it down," Nina said.

"One thing I did notice, however. Most of the killers turned out to be spouses, who had intimate knowledge of the deceased's schmearing habits."

"That doesn't help. Barry wasn't married."

"Was he intimate with anyone?"

"You might say that."

"Well, that should narrow it down."

"Not really."

"What do you mean?" Laura asked.

Nina sighed. How do you explain to two people who had

gotten engaged as undergraduates that there was still a seg-
ment of the population whose primary activity was the seduction of semistrangers? Forget it. "How about some more of
that iced tea, Laura? I think it would be delicious with a little
vodka in it."

CHAPTER 21

Nina returned to Davis Park during another rainstorm. And, of course, to a full house. "Guess where we're going," Cheryl said as soon as she walked through the door.

"Where?"

"Queens Boulevard."

"Why are we going to Queens Boulevard?"

"Because we're going to Barry's funeral."

"All of us?"

"All of us."

"Including me?"

"Well, it's up to you," Cheryl said, in a tone of voice that indicated clearly that it was hardly up to Nina at all.

"Did we get invited?"

"Barry's mother called. She said she knew what a big part Davis Park played in her son's life and she thought we should all be at the funeral. That he would have wanted it that way."

"What time is the funeral?" Nina asked.

"Two o'clock. Which means we've got to leave in about twenty minutes. You're going in Charlie's car with Ira and Jonathan. And you're wearing my black sundress with your black-and-white cardigan."

"I am?"

"What other choice do you have? You can't go to a funeral in boxer shorts."

Cheryl was right. Nina had filled her bag with flimsy, undignified garments that would keep her banned from any cathedral in Italy, as well as a Queens Boulevard Jewish funeral parlor. Cheryl's black sundress was a little bit slutty also, but under Nina's cotton cardigan, she supposed it would do. Luckily, the skirt was long and full and the top had a high spandex content, eliminating the danger of a popped button or burst seam.

"But what are you going to wear?" she asked Cheryl. "I don't want to hog your only good funeral outfit."

"My jumpsuit. With my black jacket."

It was the jumpsuit that Nina had borrowed to wear to last Friday night's party. The last time she had seen Barry. A wave of sadness hit her. Not a big one, and not an unadulterated one. The sadness was mixed with a lot of other emotions, not all sympathetic ones. But for perhaps the first time, Nina became aware of the fact that another human being had died. She thought about what Harriet had said about Barry's being terrific with the kids he taught, about them being crazy about him. And she pictured Barry dropping his arm-squeezing veneer and going off to Bushwick to do battle with the forces of evil every day. What would happen in September, when everyone would be running around asking, "Yo, where's Mr. Adelman?"

What if this had happened to her? Would the old ladies be sitting in the waiting room of Legal Services for the Elderly asking, "*Nu*, where's Ms. Fischman?" Whether it was *yo* or *nu,* the sense of loss would probably be temporary. Because when you were in public service, the needs were endless and the clients insatiable. And if you missed a step while slogging through . . . well, the public was always willing to take their business elsewhere. If they could find an elsewhere.

She stuffed herself into Cheryl's sundress, which bore an alarming resemblance to a sausage casing, and minimized the damage with her cardigan. She added some brown eyeshadow and underlined her eyes with a dark pencil. Her eyes were one of her better features, and Nina dutifully applied her pencil often, as if emphasizing a particularly noteworthy portion of a sentence or paragraph.

Earrings, the thinking woman's accessory, went on next. Like many women of her station in life, Nina traveled with a full selection. She might run out of clean underwear, but she was never without a fresh change of earrings. She rejected several of her more whimsical pairs, including a set of dangling teacups, and settled on a pair of sedate cloisonné buttons.

Her lipstick was a little bright for the occasion, but at least it had a matte finish. Apparently it was no longer desirable to sport a glossy sheen on your mouth. She had been told this by a woman who knew, and Nina took the advice to heart. She was thrilled to be in the cosmetic vanguard for once.

By the time she got upstairs, Jonathan was waiting in the living room. He was wearing a jacket and tie. Nina wondered where he got them from. Even the people on the Island who regularly worshiped at religious services wore shorts and pullovers. What kind of person kept a jacket and tie on Fire Island? She must have been looking at him somewhat suspiciously, because he offered an immediate explanation. "My father's," he said, flipping the tie between his fingers. "He always keeps a good chunk of his wardrobe on the boat."

That was the thing about rich kids, Nina thought. Their

parents afforded them backup. If you needed to borrow a car or store some boxes, they were there for you. She knew that her parents had been generous in their own way. But when she was growing up, it seemed that the only thing there was extra of in the Fischman household was insight and cynical humor. And sometimes she felt that she would have traded in a hefty helping of perspective for a parental attic.

"Nice tie," Nina said. It had things that looked like French horns all over it.

"Yeah, my father's a tie freak." Nina tried to remember her father ever having bought a tie, but she couldn't. Her father's ties always seemed to materialize out of nowhere, five years and two inches out of date. Leo Fischman had been the antithesis of a tie freak.

"I've been told that we're going in Charlie's car. Is that right?"

"Yeah," he said. "I took the boat out, so I left my car at my parents' place."

Not only did you get to leave your boxes in their attic, but you got to park your car in their driveway as well. And not only that, but your car was probably something with air-conditioning and power windows and door locks and an antilock braking system that your father let you inherit instead of trading it in. Not like the little stripped-down subcompacts that her borough friends had to pay off on time.

Like Charlie's car. There was nothing wrong with it, really. It was a cute little Honda Civic in an appealing shade of light green. And the backseat, if not exactly commodious, was big enough to accommodate the relationship that Jonathan and Nina had developed so far. But the Honda had an interior that conveyed a clear message that every upcharge had to be carefully considered.

Jonathan was quiet during the trip from Patchogue to Queens. At first Nina, following her usual instincts, took the silence personally. There was something about men in cars that usually proved unsatisfactory. Nina's expectation was that being together in a moving vehicle should prod the conversation to new heights of intimacy. Though the truth was that car rides were more likely to be boring, with long silences occasionally punctuated by requests for quarters at approaches to toll plazas.

Nina's initial sense of disappointment was gradually replaced by a feeling of unease. Was Jonathan's silence a sign of guilt? How would it feel to be attending the funeral of someone whose murder you had just arranged? But that was ridiculous, she remembered, before her imagination ran away with itself. It was perfectly normal, she thought, when you were on your way to your oldest friend's funeral, to be a little subdued. After all, how had she felt a few years back when she had gone up to the Bronx for Susan Gold's funeral? Upset, to say the least, though not quite monosyllabic. Nina could never remember an occasion that had rendered her monosyllabic. For that, she'd probably have to remember all the way back to her days in utero.

The funeral parlor looked vaguely familiar, but Nina might have been imagining it. She could have been there for a great-uncle or something, but she wasn't sure. Queens Boulevard always confused her. It cut an enormously long swath through the borough and she could never recall how to line up the neighborhoods—was it Rego Park, Forest Hills, and then Kew Gardens to the east? Or had she reversed them? The whole stretch looked the same—mostly populated by bagel stores and elderly white people, the men in short-sleeved shirts and the women carrying bags of fruit. The indigenous population seemed to eat a lot of grapes. It wasn't all that different from the main shopping street of Nina's Bronx childhood, where people also had seemed to eat a lot of grapes. The only thing missing was the elevated subway train, which loomed large in Nina's early memories, like the shadow of a giant *Tyrannosaurus rex* over the neighborhood.

If Nina hadn't been to that exact funeral parlor before, she might very well have attended a memorial service or wedding of an Adelman, since the crowd also looked vaguely, if not specifically, familiar. The mix of borough and suburban Jews was one she had witnessed dozens of times—from the far eastern reaches of the Huntington Townhouse all the way up to the lofty summit of Abigail Kirsch at Tarrytown. And at all the funeral parlors in between.

The only thing different here were the women. Not the aunts and cousins, who were your standard Loehmann's shoppers. But the young women. There must have been dozens of them. Truffaut had made a movie about this. She couldn't summon up the name of the film, but Nina remembered all the women standing around a cemetery with raised umbrellas. They were French and all had great legs and were bidding adieu to some womanizer who had died a premature death.

The women here in Queens had pretty good legs, too, but what fascinated Nina most about the group was its pan-ethnic, pan-generational, pan-socioeconomic quality. There were hot little numbers in short black dresses with cutout shoulders that looked like they must be excellent salsa dancers. And there were schoolteacher types, perhaps Barry's colleagues, who wore their summer shifts at a modest length and their sexuality coiled tightly beneath them. There were private-school types with black velvet headbands and borough girls with really big hair. The only thing they had in common was that they were all carefully checking each other out.

As they waited for the signal to file into the chapel, Nina found herself intrigued by the unlikely conversational coupling of a salsa dancer with a velvet headband. She took a few steps backward to be able to hear what those two were discussing.

"I simply can't believe it," the velvet headband was saying.

"I can," the salsa dancer replied.

"What do you think happened?"

"Which one of us did it? Is that what you mean?"

The velvet headband gave a wicked laugh in response, but Nina didn't get to hear anything further, since Jonathan appeared and pulled her over to the other side of the room. "Do you want to meet Mrs. Adelman?" he asked.

"Okay." Not that she really wanted to go through an obligatory conversation with the woman. But she was curious to see the kind of mother who would raise a son with Barry's proclivities.

Mrs. Adelman looked pretty much your run-of-the-mill Florida widow. Tan skin so wrinkled that it looked like a piece of tinfoil that had been crumpled up and then smoothed out again. She was wearing a black dress, a little slinky and showing just the tiniest top of a freckly chest. Big clip earrings that looked like crouching toads, coral lipstick and matching nails, hair dyed a too-blond shade that Nina imagined might prevail in the environs of Broward County. But it was her shoes that were shocking. They were mulelike affairs, but instead of high heels, they rested on silver balls the size of small purple plums.

Nina was always sensitive to the height of a woman's heel, having grown up with a mother whose shoe wardrobe had run the gamut of space shoes to New Balance. Nina herself, having inherited Ida's platypus feet, had to confine herself to whatever Harry's Shoes carried in a wide width. So it was inevitable that high heels would have all sorts of threatening connotations. But these little silver balls . . . well, they opened up all sorts of new vistas in familial sociopathy.

"Nina Fischman, meet Sylvia Adelman." Jonathan made the introductions in a respectful voice.

"My deepest condolences," Nina said, meaning it, but also having a hard time not staring at Mrs. Adelman's shoes. "We were all extremely shocked."

"You were? I wasn't."

"You weren't?"

"No, not really." Sylvia Adelman put a tan, wrinkly hand over her heart. "You know a mother always worries about a child. From birth. Are they eating, are they peeing, do they have other little friends to play with? Every mother goes through that. But Barry always gave me more than my share to worry about."

"Why was that?" Nina asked.

"The girls. They used to fight over him. Even in second grade. Later on, we'd get all kinds of phony phone calls and anonymous mail. We had girls waiting outside our apartment all the time. I wish I could say I never thought it would end like this, but I can't. The thought that there was serious trouble down the line crossed my mind more than once."

"So you think that Barry's death was a direct result of his . . . er . . . complicated love life?"

"I'm sure of it." Sylvia Adelman's voice lowered to a more thoughtful tone. "It's funny, isn't it? All the trouble that's out there for sons like mine—the drugs, the gambling, the white-collar crime. And my Barry sticks with women. Such an old-fashioned vice."

An old-fashioned vice. But a deadly one? The salsa dancer and the velvet headband might be sure of it, but Nina wasn't thoroughly convinced. But for the rest of the day, all the way back to Patchogue, through rush hour traffic on the

Long Island Expressway and a crowded ferry ride, Nina kept thinking of Sylvia Adelman and the way she had said "such an old-fashioned vice." With sadness and deep regret. But also with a little bit of pride.

CHAPTER 22

"Well, that was a very interesting funeral," Cheryl said later that day, back in Davis Park. "And to think, we almost missed it." She was sitting in front of the television with Nina and Harriet watching a videotape of an old *Seinfeld* episode. The show was developing quite a cult following. Perhaps, in the future, there would be conventions like the ones filled with people obsessed with *The Honeymooners* or *Star Trek,* who dressed up like the characters and could recite every word to every episode.

"How did we almost miss it?" Nina asked.

Cheryl sat silently for a moment while she watched Kramer's hair catch on fire. "When Barry's mother called the house," she finally answered, "I talked to her. She said that she was planning at first to have a private graveside ceremony for family only. Then she changed her mind at the last minute. But I don't know that I believe her."

"What do you mean?"

"I think she was planning a funeral all along but didn't want anyone from Fire Island there," Cheryl said. "After all, you saw how many people were at the funeral. You can't get the word out that quickly at the last minute and have such a turnout."

"Why would she not want to invite us?"

"Because she's suspicious. She thinks one of us did it. And I don't necessarily disagree with her."

"That's a terrible thing to say, Cheryl." Harriet sounded genuinely upset. "What happened to all that stuff about the people in the house sticking together?"

"I said I thought someone in Fire Island might be guilty. Not someone in the house."

"And what is that supposed to mean?" asked Harriet.

Nina didn't want to hear anything negative about Jonathan. She wasn't in the mood for cognitive dissonance.

"Well, Mrs. Adelman had something very interesting to say when I spoke with her on the phone. Unfortunately, I did not get a chance to pursue the conversation with her at the funeral."

"What did she say over the phone?"

"It seems that the police are looking for someone from Canada. That the box of patches that Barry was using was only sold in Canada. And you know whose family has a house up there, don't you?"

"Whose?" asked Harriet.

Cheryl just sat there, looking at Nina, with her eyebrows arched all the way up to her hairline.

"She's talking about Jonathan," Nina said.

"You can't honestly believe that Jonathan had anything to do with Barry's death," Harriet said.

"I do and I have for some time."

That was interesting, thought Nina. She thinks he's a murderer, but that hasn't stopped her from encouraging me to get involved with him. It was a little hard to explain. Maybe she was lying, trying to seem more clever than she is, and the thought that Jonathan might be guilty hadn't occurred to her until she talked to Mrs. Adelman. Or maybe the market was so bad that an available man was worth pursuing even if he did have homicidal tendencies.

Was Cheryl's desire to make a *shiddoch* so strong that the small matter of a murder got overlooked? And if so, why? In Nina's experience, it was married people that tried to fix you up all the time. To get you to come over to their side. Single people didn't bother. After all, you didn't see Christians running around trying to convert people to Judaism, did you? Or vice versa, except for those Jews for Jesus people, and they were a very small band of serious nut cases.

Was Cheryl that nuts? She was certainly controlling. She treated people like chess pieces. Maybe she was just playing a game, idly manipulating Nina and Jonathan to see what would happen. Or playing a hunch and wanting to prove herself right. Whichever, Cheryl's intentions were probably not evil.

Besides, Nina didn't really believe that Jonathan murdered Barry. The line between neurotic and sociopathic was not, in her experience, a fine one. And Nina was sure that Jonathan was not inclined to cross over.

"It's up to you to find out what really happened." Cheryl used her strict schoolmistress voice.

"Are you talking to me?" Nina asked.

"Of course I am."

"Why me?"

"Because Jonathan likes you. He'll open up to you in a way that he won't to the rest of us."

"But he seems like a really open guy," Harriet said. "It's hard to believe that he's hiding anything."

"Thank you," Nina said. "I was beginning to question my perceptions."

"Don't take everything at face value. The nicest guy in the world can turn out to be a shit." Cheryl had moved on from strict schoolmistress to fascist dictator. "You both know that's true. Don't tell me that you don't agree. No woman can remain single as long as we have and not have learned that firsthand."

Nina thought back to all the nice guys she dated that had turned into disappearing acts. She wasn't sure that exactly made them shits, or capable of murder. But it did seem they were capable of at least a certain level of deceit. Nina flipped through her mental Rolodex of failed relationships. Many of them had seemed devoted and attentive up until the very end. And the end was always so abrupt. Although truthfully, when she let herself be a Monday morning quarterback, she had to admit that she had seen it coming, at least a little.

But the methods they chose were so rude—usually a phone call or sometimes no phone call at all, just a large, gaping silence. She felt that Jonathan was different. But then, how many times had she told herself just that, starting out?

"Am I right or what?" Cheryl snapped.

Harriet just sat there, looking cowed and miserable. She shrugged.

"I guess so," Nina said. "But if we believe that, how are we supposed to go on?"

"I don't have an answer for that," Cheryl said. "But I do know that it's important to protect yourself."

"I don't understand," Nina said. "During the weekend you were all gung ho for me to hook up with Jonathan. You said we were perfect for each other. Now you're telling me to wear a gas mask. I don't get it."

"In many ways you are perfect for each other. But that doesn't mean he didn't murder Barry. Look, maybe I'm wrong. Maybe he didn't. Maybe you will hook up with him. And I'll wish you all the best—a short course of couple's therapy and a long and satisfying marriage. But it's up to you to find out what you're destined for. And I do think that before you get more involved with him, you should resolve the issue of whether or not he's committed homicide."

Nina returned her attention to the television. Seinfeld et al were sitting in their usual coffee shop hangout. The interior was obviously filmed in L.A., but the exterior shot was a genuine one of a place up on Broadway and 112th Street. She herself had put time in there, agonizing over the same kind of idiocy that the television characters did. She recalled a three-hour breakfast marathon one Saturday morning years ago. She and a friend had conducted an exhaustive postmortem on a first date that Nina had the night before. As it turned out, it had been a wasted three hours, since the only time Nina ever heard his voice again was on his message machine.

She was sick of wasting three hours discussing phantom men. She was ready to move the plot along, but she just didn't know how. Jonathan held out some promise, but now he seemed potentially dangerous. She had to admit that he was the only one around who had a real motive for murdering Barry. If she believed what she heard, Barry had slept with Jonathan's wife, played around with his money, and lost his *Mad* magazines. It was the kind of sick relationship that needed to be torn out by the roots. But the roots grew so deep that it could not have been easy to end it. Nina understood relationships like that. Sometimes murder was the only way out.

Maybe Cheryl was right. There really was no one else who made such a good suspect. Nina considered packing up and going back to the city. The rainy weather would scarcely be noticeable in Manhattan. And she just didn't have the heart to devote the rest of her vacation to exposing Jonathan Harris as a cold-blooded killer.

"Are you seeing him again?" Cheryl asked.

"He sort of said something about tonight."

"Good."

"But I was thinking of going back to town," Nina said. "What with this crummy weather and all."

"That's right. Leave us all here to investigate this murder by ourselves."

"Oh, please." Cheryl wasn't as good manipulating by guilt as she was by sheer domination. Usually people were good at one or the other, rarely both.

"Don't leave," Harriet said. "It's supposed to clear up to-morrow. Besides, Charlie went back over to the mainland to get lobsters for dinner. And he's getting one for you."

"That was awfully nice of him. How did you get him to do that?" Nina asked.

"We promised him we'd all eat the salad course last."

"Very clever."

"Please stay," Harriet said. "I have a whole season's worth of *Seinfeld* on tape."

Seinfeld and lobster. It didn't get much better than that. She'd stay. Besides, Cheryl would kill her if she left.

CHAPTER 23

If Nina wasn't going back to the city, maybe she'd give her mother a call to see how she was doing. Ida Fischman was pretty much always the same. Not getting any younger, thank you very much, but fine, just fine.

Although as Ida slipped more firmly into her seventies, she was evidencing a tendency to conversationally explore the world of physical ailments more and more. And not only her own. She had moved on to discussing people that Nina had never even met. This worried her daughter, who had always admired her mother for her sense of audience.

Not that Ida had really lost her sense of audience. But she had become somewhat conversationally self-indulgent. She knew that what she was saying wasn't inherently interesting, but she just couldn't resist. She was an old lady, and if she felt like talking about someone's gall bladder, goddamnit, she was going to do just that.

Nina hoped never to be afflicted with this syndrome. But

she knew she would be. Because she was already that way. Not about physical ailments, but about psychological ones. Nina could not stop herself from going on and on about someone's neurotic behavior, even if she was describing a stranger to the person listening. Sometimes Nina didn't even know the person she was talking about. And she knew that it was only a matter of time before the psychological took a turn to the medical.

She had told her mother that Ida's pattern of behavior was annoying, had even tried to set a three-minute time limit on all medical topics. When it came to pointing out annoying tendencies, Nina was right on Ida's case. It was, Nina suspected, an inevitable dynamic in any mother-daughter relationship, no matter how good. And Nina had always considered their relationship to be a good one. She hadn't hit it big in the sweepstakes of life, but she had received both a good head of hair and a good mother. Not that she had appreciated either in the early years, when thin and blond was in vogue for hair and mothers. But over time, Nina had begun to be grateful for both.

Ida had something that distinguished her from many of Nina's friends' mothers. Which was that most of the time she made sense. Nina never had to alter her tone of voice when she spoke to her, or circumscribe the subject matter or play to her mother in any particular way. She could talk to her like she would talk to any other reasonable and well-informed person, and expect to get a rational response. This, Nina had come to realize, was a blessing.

So if Ida wanted to give herself a little treat and talk about Pauline Halpern's husband's gall bladder for a while, so be it. Listening was a small price to pay for a mother who didn't make you feel worthless for being single and, as an extra added bonus, could also discuss contemporary women's fiction.

Nina waited until everyone else had drifted out onto the deck before she made the call. It wasn't as if she wanted to hide anything. Calling your mother was something everyone did, but they did it in private, like clipping their toenails.

The phone rang several times before Ida picked up. "I was in the bathroom," she explained, "seizing the moment."

Nina sensed the possibility that a gastrointestinal conversation might be about to ensue and tried to distract Ida. "How's the weather in the city? It sucks out here." Nina still tended to use the vocabulary she had learned at Camp Wel-Met in her conversations with her mother. It was infantile, she knew, but wasn't that what parents were for? To regress in front of?

"I wouldn't exactly call it a beach day," Ida said. "We had a lot of rain this morning, but it seems to be subsiding. How is your vacation going?"

"Well, we've had a bit of trouble."

"What's wrong?"

"Someone was murdered out here during the weekend."

"Someone you knew?"

"Sort of."

"Yes or no?"

"He had a share in this house. He was the house organizer, actually."

"My God. What happened?"

"You'll never believe this one."

"Try me," Ida said. "I'm starting to feel like I've been around."

"That's true. Nothing will ever top Mrs. Gross and the cockroach powder. But this comes close. This guy was supposed to go sailing on Saturday morning. So Friday night, before he went to bed, he put one of those transdermal patches on, behind his ear. So he wouldn't get seasick on the boat. Someone apparently tampered with the patch."

"In what way?"

"Put a toxic substance on it that was transmitted through his skin."

"Poison? They poisoned it? With what?"

"I don't know. The police haven't exactly issued a memo to the general public. I've pieced together the story by listening to local gossip."

"That's usually best."

Nina could just picture her mother nodding gravely. "It is, isn't it?"

"So do the local gossips have any idea who did it?" Ida asked. "Or why?"

"It's unclear. Things are complicated by the fact that Barry, the guy who was killed, was a loathsome womanizer who had screwed over practically every female in town."

"Including you?"

"Ma, I just got here. Whaddaya think, that I got off the ferry and jumped into this guy's bed?"

"I never know what to think." Ida sounded arch.

"Oh, please. Spare me the fallen-woman routine. You know that I spend most of my evenings washing pantyhose and trying to catch up on back issues of the *New Yorker*. Although less so, since Tina Brown took over."

"Really? Do you see that much of a difference? Does it really bother you?"

"A little." It was more than a little, actually. *The New Yorker* had been the one magazine that had straddled nerdiness and glitz in the same way that Nina straddled the two. It used to be a magazine that could be read by both academics who lived in small college towns and still wore Wallabees and women who wore Chanel suits and ate lunch at Bice. Tina Brown had tipped the magazine irrevocably toward the Bice bunch and Nina missed the old nerdy qualities. All those little articles about some weird smelly man who had inherited his father's ravioli business or some nutty science fiction writer who publishes a book a week had been replaced by celeb bios.

However, she wasn't in the mood for a full-blown discussion about this right now. It was a long-distance call and sooner or later someone would come in from the deck and she'd have to get off. "Anyway," Nina continued, "I never slept with him, but everyone else in the house seems to have indulged."

"You're kidding. What kind of place are you staying in? A cathouse?"

"Hardly. Although we can get a little catty at times."

"Seriously, Nina, I don't understand. Every woman in the house slept with the same man? And they all act like everything's just fine, and get up and drink coffee together in the morning?"

"Something like that."

"And then one day he just doesn't get up?"

"Exactly."

"Jesus, I know that my generation had its problems, what with sexual repression and girdles and all. But do you honestly consider this progress?"

"I don't know," Nina said. "Girdles are back, by the way. Except they're marketing them as slips with extra-firm control."

"I know, I've seen the ads. But don't change the subject. How did you end up in that place to begin with?"

"Cheryl Schneiderman. From my office. Her friend left the house, so she asked me if I wanted to take her place."

"Which one is Cheryl? The one with the crew cut?"

"Her hair isn't so short now. It's sort of . . . well, it's more normal."

"I only met her once," Ida said. "When you got that award."

"The one for ten years of dedicated masochism." Nina

and a dozen other attorneys had been presented with a certif-
icate of merit for a decade of devoted service to various New
York City legal services offices. There was a lot of turnover in
the legal services program and only a hardy few could stick
out an entire decade. Nina had suggested to the other recipi-
ents that they all form a therapy group.

"Cheryl looked a little severe, if I recall," Ida said. "Was
she sexually involved with this man also?"

"Yeah."

"I'm surprised."

"Why?" Nina asked. "Just because she had a short haircut doesn't mean she's gay."

"I didn't mean that. She just didn't seem like the type
who would sit there and watch someone she used to date
wander from bedroom to bedroom."

Her mother was right. "That's true. Cheryl is hard on
men. She usually doesn't have much tolerance for that kind
of behavior. I think she had a terrible relationship with her
father."

"In what way?" Ida asked.

Nina was encouraged that her mother was still willing to
discuss the psychological, that gall bladders hadn't completely
taken over as a topic of conversation. "Her parents were divorced when she was fairly young—early adolescence, I
think. And her father pretty much disappeared for a couple
of years. He seems to have skipped out on his child support
payments along with his visitations. Once she went away to
college, I think he showed up again and they were able to
maintain some sort of relationship. But I don't know how
good it was. And believe me, it shows."

"Meaning what?"

"Cheryl hasn't had the easiest time getting involved with
men. Not that anybody I know has. Except for your younger

daughter, of course. But in my crowd, it's been tough for all of us."

"And Cheryl?"

"It's not like she never goes out with anybody. For one thing, she's attractive, so that makes it easier."

"She's attractive if you're into bald women."

"No, Ma. Really, she looks pretty good. And she's outgoing. Well, I don't know if you'd call it outgoing, but she's certainly not shy."

"That I'll believe."

"So there's often someone new on the horizon, but things always end badly. Ugly, messy terminations. That's why I was surprised about Barry."

"The one who got killed?"

"Yeah. She was apparently sleeping with him last summer and then they broke up."

"Talk about ugly, messy terminations," Ida said. "The poor guy."

"No, it wasn't like that. They stayed really close friends. It was unusual."

"I'll say. How many of your old boyfriends are you talking to?"

"None," admitted Nina. "Actually, I don't even seem to be talking to my present one."

"Trouble in paradise?"

"You might say that."

"What's wrong?"

"I'm too old to be telling my mother about my romantic problems. Besides, it's no big deal. Tom decided to spend his vacation with his daughter instead of me. He's entitled."

"Well, maybe you can look around Fire Island for someone more appropriate."

Appropriate. It was a favorite word of many mothers and it meant something different to each one. To some it meant

Jewish, to some it meant rich, to some it meant not having any child support obligations. But Nina didn't think it meant any of these things to Ida. To her mother it meant someone who was ready to spend the rest of his life hanging around the house with you. And Nina had to admit that it didn't seem as misguided as it used to.

"Yeah, well, maybe." Nina sighed. "Look, I'm gonna go."

"How long are you staying out there?"

"I'll be back Sunday. Bye." Nina hung up, relieved that they had gotten through the conversation without any mention of gall bladders. But haunted, somehow, by that word her mother had used. Was Jonathan more appropriate than Tom? Maybe. But that probably depended on whether or not he had killed Barry.

CHAPTER 24

Lobster dinners were always exciting events. Even though Nina knew they were really *schmutz*-eating, bottom-dwelling creatures that her ancestors had been smart enough to steer clear of. And that up in Maine, where they were considered the insects of the sea, a native that had grown up in a lobsterman's family would sometimes retch at the very smell.

But in Davis Park, as in all the cities and suburbs across America, there was nothing more desirable than plunging a living, struggling creature to its death in boiling water and then ripping it apart with the aid of various tools of dismemberment. And Nina was an expert dismemberer. At eight dollars a pound, she could justify leaving no shred uneaten.

The entire household was so grateful to Charlie for fetching the creatures that not only did they save the salad course for last, but they knocked themselves out on a salade composée so intricate that it was guaranteed to make any Italian American yuppie happy. Nancy toasted pignolias and Estelle brought out some radish sprouts that she had been cultivating for weeks. Ira paid a visit to Kevin the kitchen Nazi and extracted a few ounces of Montrachet laced with cracked peppercorns. Kevin only agreed to part with it after Ira promised to warm the goat cheese before sprinkling it on top of the salad.

Cheryl conned a neighbor out of some mache, a lettuce so soft that you could stuff quilts with it. And instead of using a pig to hunt truffles, the house sent Harriet off to track down some wild mushrooms. She was able to score a handful of fresh porcini without difficulty, since there were so many people in town that owed her favors. The pièce de résistance, however, was a hunk of pancetta that Barbara had been saving for God-knew-what occasion. The bacon was diced and sautéed until crisp and then spread on top of the salad along with Kevin's crumbled warm Montrachet.

Jonathan came over in the middle of the salad course. He readily identified the pine nuts, and even diagnosed them as toasted. He knew that the mushrooms were wild without pinpointing them as porcini. The pancetta and Montrachet eluded him completely. He guessed Canadian bacon and Roquefort and didn't even notice the radish sprouts.

Nina was pleased with his perceptions. He showed a reasonably wide scope of knowledge, without being a prig. She wasn't looking for a man who could pull a crumb of cheese out of the salad, roll it around his palate and pronounce "Aha! Montrachet! Domestic, I believe. Perhaps from Coach Farms?" She had gone out with enough of those types, with their unblended Scotches and their Parma ham and their forty-dollar bottles of balsamic vinegar, to know to steer clear. On the other hand, she wasn't looking for a man with a Budweiser can grafted onto his palm either.

She realized how little she knew about Jonathan. He had, like most products of psychotherapy, talked mostly about his early years. She didn't even know his zip code. And Nina was a zip code fanatic. It told volumes about a person: more than their sun, moon, and rising signs put together. She supposed she should find out what the story was with his career. She was definitely behind schedule on that one.

"Who's up for a trip to the Casino?" Barbara asked.

"Everybody," answered Cheryl. The others nodded their assent. It reminded Nina of her freshman year in the dorm, when someone would shout "Time for dinner" and fourteen women would head for the cafeteria in lockstep.

"How about if we stay here and clean up?" Jonathan asked Nina.

"Fine." She was relieved. Also apprehensive. She hadn't been in an empty house with Jonathan yet. Actually, she hadn't been in an empty house at all since she got here. The constant company was unnerving. She tried to calm herself and prepare for some sort of denouement.

Later, after everyone had left and Jonathan and Nina were clearing the table, a somewhat tense silence descended. Nina broke it with some idiocy about wasn't it a shame to throw out all these lovely lobster shells and should she make a stock or something.

"Why?" Jonathan asked. "Do you need lobster stock for a recipe?"

"No, of course not. It's just hard for me to throw anything out." She spared him a lengthy description of the laddered pantyhose and shredded towels and decade-old herbal teas that cluttered her apartment. "Waste not, want not. Take care of the pence and the pounds will take care of themselves."

"I guess." Jonathan shrugged.

"After all, we never threw out anything in the Bronx. That's where I grew up."

"It is?"

So he hadn't been listening all this time. Wait a minute, was it possible that she actually hadn't raised the topic in conversation? Nina tried to recall her dialogues with Jonathan. She couldn't actually remember uttering the word *Bronx*. This constituted some kind of breakthrough. Usually it was the first word out of her mouth, as if to put the listener on notice that they were not to expect her to speak in well-modulated tones and cross her legs like a lady and indulge in nostalgic chats about tailgate picnics and high school football games. (Bronx Science hadn't even had a team.)

Maybe she was getting less defensive in her later years. "It is?" he had said. Had he said it snottily or judgmentally? She filtered his tone of voice through her paranoidometer. He came out okay.

"Yup," she said. "The Bronx. And I mean the real thing. Not Riverdale."

"I'm not surprised."

Uh-oh. "How come?" she asked, trying desperately to smooth out the edges in her voice.

"Because you're funny. You know, there's an old theory that people who grew up in the Bronx were funnier than people who grew up in Brooklyn. And that the closer to the Grand Concourse you lived, the funnier you were."

First he tells her she's not fat, then he tells her she's funny. The guy might be the greatest discovery of the twentieth century since the planet Pluto.

"I don't know if I buy that bit about the Grand Concourse," Nina said, plunging her hands into a sink filled with dirty dishes and lobster crud. "The East Bronx has had to live in the shadow of the Concourse for too long. It's unfair. Some very famous people lived in the East Bronx."

"Such as?"

"Trotsky lived on Vyse Avenue for a while. In the twenties, I think."

"Trotsky. A very funny guy. Did you ever catch his act in the mountains?"

"Yeah, well, we might as well be talking about the lost continent of Atlantis. It takes more than just a sense of humor to grow up on Vyse Avenue these days."

"I know," he said. "I do volunteer work with elementary school kids at P.S. 30 in Mott Haven." Mott Haven was really the real thing. As far from Riverdale as you could get.

"What kind of volunteer work?"

"An after-school art program."

"Are you an artist?"

"Yeah, an illustrator."

The guy was an artist, found her weight acceptable, did volunteer work, and thought she was funny. And he wasn't married or gay. In that case he *must* have killed Barry.

"Let me ask you something," she said, handing him a dish to dry. "I heard a new piece of information about Barry's death. Something about Canada. That they had traced the patch that he used to Canada. Have you been up to your family's house in Nova Scotia lately?"

He put down the dish and sat down at the dining room table. "Dry your hands off and sit down for a minute. I have to talk to you about something."

Here it comes, she thought. The part of the story that ends with Nina saying, "I knew it was too good to be true."

"I gave Jonathan that box of transdermal patches he was using. I had been keeping him in patches for years. You see, they're an over-the-counter drug in Canada. You still need a prescription to get them in the States. So whenever I was up in Nova Scotia, I would bring Barry back a couple of boxes. That way, when we brought women on the boat, he wouldn't have to interrupt his seduction routine by retching."

"And? What does this mean?"

"What do you mean?"

"Are you trying to tell me that you were responsible for his death?" Now there was a euphemism if she ever heard one.

"You don't think that I poisoned him, do you?"

"What am I supposed to think?"

"Look, Nina, I swear I never opened that box. I bought it in a drugstore in Halifax and never opened it."

"Do the police know about this?" she asked.

"Of course. I had to tell them."

Now came the hard part, whether or not to believe him. She could usually tell when someone was lying, but she had a harder time figuring out if someone was telling the truth.

CHAPTER 25

"I just don't know whether or not I can trust you," Nina said, because she really didn't.

"Oh, God. I can't believe any of this is happening." Jonathan put his hands over his face.

It was all she could do to keep from wrapping her arms around him. That seemed to be the way life always was. You had to keep yourself from wrapping your arms around some man for some reason: he would find it threatening, or you had broken up with him last week, or the two of you were just friends. This was a rather unusual case, a first: you had to keep your hands off him until you figured out whether or not he had murdered someone last Friday night.

"Look," she said. "Let's talk this through. When did you give Barry that box of motion-sickness patches?"

"Last September, I think. I went up to Canada in August and came back with two boxes for him. Dad brought the boat back sometime the next month and I took Barry out for a sail a couple of weeks after that. I gave both boxes to him the day before, so he could put one on that night and not have to wait for it to kick in the next morning."

"And he was still using the same box this summer?"

"That or the other one I gave him. There are only two patches to a box, but I don't think he had any use for them in the winter. I mean, it's not like he was the kind of guy who took his Christmas vacations on the QE2."

"Are you sure?"

"Well, I really have no way of knowing. I assume that he was still using the patches I gave him."

"Were there expiration dates on the boxes you gave him?"

"I didn't check or anything. But I seem to remember that the boxes do have expiration dates."

"How are these things packaged?"

"As I said, two to a box. And each patch is separately wrapped in a tinfoil pouch. You peel away the sides to get the patch out."

"Is there a separate expiration date on each patch?"

"I don't know. Why?"

"Because if someone tampered with a patch and then used it to replace one of the patches in Barry's box, it might have a different expiration date than the one on the box."

"It might," Jonathan said. "Did the police find the wrapper?"

"I don't know. They definitely went through the garbage. That I remember."

"Look, I'm sorry you had to get involved in this mess, Nina. I mean, I wish we could have met under better circumstances. Because I think we have something." He paused. "Special," he added.

How sweet, she thought. Special was always a hard word to say. In fact, it made her a little uncomfortable. "Yeah," she said, "getting involved with someone is hard enough, without having to wonder whether or not they're guilty of homicide." Had she said that aloud? Nina surprised herself. It was as if one of her endless interior monologues had developed a life of its own and decided to come out of the closet.

"Nina, I didn't murder Barry."

"How can I know that for sure?"

"Because if I was going to kill him, I would have killed him a long time ago."

"Oh, great, that's a real comfort. Your main alibi is that you've felt like killing him for years."

"But it's true," Jonathan said. "When I was younger, I was so much more tortured. I didn't need Barry to make me feel inadequate. But he made things worse. And for some reason I could never end the relationship. Now I understand why."

"Why couldn't you?"

"Because in lots of ways I got a tremendous kick out of him. He had some terrible qualities, but he also had so much energy and imagination. Whenever I felt like I was living my life in black and white, I'd call up Barry and it was like instant Technicolor. It took me quite a long time to be able to appreciate him without mixing in a lot of anger. It wasn't until I turned forty that I felt like I could really handle him, that our friendship wasn't based solely on my neuroses."

"I see." Nina knew what he meant, but she couldn't tell if he was bullshitting her or not. After all, he might just be cleverly and demonically playing to his audience, knowing that Nina was a sucker for a plot that featured neurosis as a leading character.

"I don't blame you for being confused," he said. "If you'd rather I stay away until this whole thing gets resolved, I'll understand."

"But I don't want you to slip through my fingers." Jesus,

she was saying things to this guy that she usually only said to herself.

He smiled. "I've been on the market for a long time. I don't see myself getting snapped up as soon as you turn your back."

"I wondered about that. Market conditions being what they are, you must have some fatal flaw that's escaping my attention." There were so many to choose from these days— he could be impotent, or HIV positive, or wanted for back taxes. Actually, maybe one casual homicide wasn't such a big deal.

"It depends on what you consider a fatal flaw. My career is a mess, and that turns a lot of women off."

"I thought you said you were in advertising."

"In and out of advertising. Out at the moment. It's a volatile field, especially in the art department. I seem to get laid off more often than Barry got laid."

Nina groaned.

"I also occasionally make bad puns," he said. "Other than that, except for having a lot of cat hair on my furniture, I'd say I'm a real catch."

A man with a cat. The thought appealed to Nina. She herself did not own a cat, since it didn't fit in with her "any minute I can split" scenario. But if she ever got together with someone, she wouldn't mind getting together with his cat as well. She had potential as a cat person. Besides, a Jewish man without allergies was a rare thing indeed.

"Cat hair on your furniture? And where might that furniture be located, if I may ask?"

"Eighty-second and Third."

Nina didn't know what to think. She had never seriously dated someone who lived on the Upper East Side. On the other hand, there was something perfect about it. The Village was charming and Chelsea was convenient, but a residence in either neighborhood could make his heterosexual status suspect. The Lower East Side was a logistical nightmare, requiring either three trains or a fifteen-dollar cab ride. And the Upper West Side . . . well, she had certainly dated plenty of men from her own neighborhood. But sometimes she felt an incipient inbreeding problem. She was tired of having the same old conversation about the lines at Carmine's and the grievous loss of the Cinema Studio and how ugly the Columbia Condominium was.

Lately she had started to feel as if she were living in a Koren cartoon. Enough was enough. Here was Jonathan, whose braided leather belt and 10028 address spoke of whole new worlds. Why fight it?

"Boy, I must really like you," she said. "Usually when someone tells me that they live in Dry Dock country, I'm out the door."

"I believe that the Dry Dock Bank has been closed for years," he said curtly. "Or merged or something. Besides, Eighty-second Street is too far north to be considered Dry Dock country."

"Well, the wrong side of the park then."

"Don't tell me you're one of those sanctimonious Upper West Siders who think that the sun rises over Central Park West and sets over Riverside Drive."

"Very poetic," she said. "No, I'm just one of those sanctimonious Upper West Siders who think any place else is the Diaspora."

"C'mon, Nina. Plenty of normal people live on the Upper East Side."

"Name one."

"Woody Allen."

"Um, I wouldn't exactly call him normal, even if nothing did happen in that attic in Connecticut. Name someone else."

"I give up."

"I'll tell you who lives on the Upper East Side," Nina said. "Ralph Lauren and Calvin Klein and a lot of other Jewish Waspophiles who try to pretend that they can't remember how to pronounce Mosholu Parkway."

"Is that what's bothering you? You think that I'm a fake WASP?"

"No, I'm just flailing around, trying to find something to be defensive about." She had to admit that this was pretty cool, having your interior monologues out loud.

"Because I think that the fake-WASP thing is a bogus issue," he said.

"I'm sure you're right. I'll admit that I'm a little nervous. Beginnings make me nervous. I mean, we haven't even slept together yet. And up until a few minutes ago, I didn't even know your zip code."

"Now that we've gotten my postal status clear, do you want to get the other thing you mentioned out of the way?"

"I don't know what to do. I guess I could handle the fact that you're unemployed and live on the wrong side of the park. But an unemployed murderer who lives on the wrong side of the park might be too much for even someone like me, who tries not to do the predictable."

"I'm not a murderer," he said, lifting her hair off her shoulders and kissing her throat.

"How can I be sure?"

"Give me a polygraph test."

Nina wondered if the Suffolk County Police would administer a polygraph to Jonathan to help her decide whether or not to go to bed with him. Probably not, even though they could use the results in their investigation.

"I just know I'm going to regret this," she said, the moment before their lips met.

CHAPTER 26

Jonathan had only gotten as far down as her collarbone, when Ira and Charlie came stomping through the door.

"Anybody home?"

"Boy, that was fast," Jonathan said, moving a few inches away from Nina but holding on to her hand.

"Yeah, well, the Casino was giving me a headache," Ira said. "I think I might have a sinus infection or something."

"Besides," said Charlie, "we're getting tired of the same old faces."

Nina was tempted to launch into her "who the hell do you think you are?" lecture. But a lesson in humility wasn't going to help these two. Both men knew damn well that the twenty-five-year-old superb physical specimens had no more interest in Charlie or Ira than they had ten years ago. And they probably knew as well that their search for the Holy Grail was pointless and if it went on much longer, they might start reminding people of Ernest Borgnine in *Marty*.

Nina figured that since they knew all that, there was no point in reminding them. They were addicted to fruitless quests after blond people and that to put an end to this behavior would require them to search deep into their souls.

So she changed the subject. "We're trying to figure out who killed Barry," she said. "Either of you guys have any ideas?"

"Yeah," Jonathan said. "It's very important that Nina find out who did it."

"How come?"

"Because she thinks it was me."

"I didn't say that." She grabbed her hand away from Jonathan. "I just said that until I had ruled you out, I didn't feel comfortable with your hands around my neck."

"You see the problem?" Jonathan asked. "I'm being shut out until I can prove my innocence. So if one of you is guilty, please confess now, so we can get on with our budding romance."

"I'd love to help you out and confess," Ira said, "but I'm due for a promotion in September, so it's a bad time to throw my life away just so that you can get laid."

"I think it was a woman," Charlie said.

"What makes you say that?" asked Nina.

"The method. Poison. It's womanish."

"And if you were going to kill Barry, you'd blow him away with an Uzi?" Nina doubted it. She suspected that Charlie was more adept with a Cuisinart than a machine gun.

"Well, I've certainly thought about killing him. Haven't you, Ira?"

"At times."

"You did?"

"Yeah," said Ira. "It's hard to stand by on the sidelines, watching Barry score time after time. It makes you feel like a loser."

"Neither of you has to feel that way." Nina couldn't help herself. "You're not losers, you're both obviously running after the wrong women."

Ira shook his head and pursed his lips. "I just don't want to settle."

Nina pictured taking a large ax and wedging it into Ira's skull. Jonathan must have sensed her agitation, because he interrupted. "Well, Charlie, if you think it's a woman, which one? Because there are plenty around."

"My money's on Mindy," Charlie said. " 'Hell hath no fury like a woman scorned.' Boy, was she pissed at Barry when he started seeing Angela. I mean, I don't exactly remember her saying 'I'll get him for this,' but whatever she did say, it was along those lines."

"No way," said Ira. "You're imagining things. You just have it in for Mindy because she jumped into bed with Barry instead of you." Ira turned to Nina. "Charlie made a big play for Mindy, but she wasn't having any."

"She *was* my type," Charlie admitted.

"And what type is that?" Nina asked.

"Sort of a cheerleader type. Mindy was very warm and friendly. Filled with energy and enthusiasm."

"Also tall and blond," Ira added.

"Your basic nightmare," Nina said.

Jonathan laughed. "Mindy was a spoiled brat from Lawrence who always got what she wanted. That's why she couldn't handle Barry's defection."

"Cedarhurst," Charlie said mournfully. "Not Lawrence. Cedarhurst."

"Whatever," said Jonathan. "I personally couldn't stand her. But I don't think she killed Barry."

"Why not?"

"For one thing, she left the house the day after she found Barry in bed with Angela. She didn't have the opportunity to plant a poisoned patch in Barry's bedroom. Unless she had an accomplice."

"Now, there's a theory," Ira said. "Any one of the women in the house might have helped her out. The obvious choices are Barbara and Cheryl, both of whom have murderous personalities. But you shouldn't underestimate Estelle, who's quiet but sharp as they come. Or Elizabeth, who's classy but vindictive."

"Or Nancy," Charlie added, "who has the temperament of a redhead. When she gets angry, watch out. And there's also Maggie."

"She wouldn't have to use poison," Ira said. "One screech and Barry would immediately succumb."

"That only leaves Harriet," Nina said.

"Ah, yes." Charlie raised his eyebrows. "Harriet. I like it. It has all the classic elements of a good murder mystery. The sweet, put-upon mousy young woman who no one in a million years would suspect. The perfect murderer."

"I thought we were still talking about Mindy," Nina said.

"Not necessarily," Ira pointed out. "I mean, maybe someone in the house acted as Mindy's accomplice. Or they could have acted alone. Either way."

"But what's the motive?" Jonathan asked.

Ira and Charlie exchanged a look. "Variations on a theme," Charlie said. "They all got dumped by him."

"Every single one of them?"

"Yup. Ask Nina. She'll tell you."

"It's true," Nina said. "Barry had an affair with each of the women in the house. Of varying duration, needless to say."

"Including you?"

"Of course not. But everyone else. Even Harriet. The problem with the revenge theory is that I don't think any one of them took Barry that seriously. Certainly not seriously enough to kill him."

"What do you mean?" asked Jonathan.

"They all seemed to be taking a 'good riddance to bad rubbish' attitude to his infidelity. Casual, not worth breaking a sweat over, much less rousing oneself to homicide. In a way, they all seemed to consider the whole thing somewhat amusing."

"I can see that," Jonathan said. "Barry was always a caveat emptor kind of guy."

"Huh?" Ira didn't get it.

"You know; Buyer beware. He was up front about his short sexual attention span. Most women knew what they were getting into. And couldn't blame him when the inevitable happened."

"That's a lot of bullshit, you know." Nina sounded louder than she meant to. "Knowing what's coming doesn't help. Men can't get off the hook with just a simple caveat emptor." She gave Jonathan a sharp look to drive the point home. Just in case he turned out to be a closet disappearer.

"I'll keep that in mind."

"So do you think that the women in the house were just pretending?" asked Charlie. "Keeping a stiff upper lip while their hearts were really broken?"

"That's an oversimplification," Nina said. "Besides, you're talking about seven different women. There's got to be a broad range of reactions. Some are more fragile than others."

"So who's your money on?" asked Charlie.

"Me? What do I know?" Nina shrugged. "I just got here last Friday. I'm still having trouble telling them apart. I have to use mnemonic devices, like Maggie the Magpie and Queen Elizabeth and Hairy Harriet."

Ira and Charlie laughed. Nina felt like a traitor. "What

about Angela?" she asked, trying to shift the focus. "I only saw her once, at the sunset party over at Sunmist, but she looked pretty scary to me."

"Yeah, Angela," Ira said. "Barry was two-timing her with Jenny."

"You're right," Charlie said. "She's fierce. I could see her seeking revenge. It's a big theme with Greeks, you know."

"It was a big theme two thousand years ago," Jonathan said.

"Believe me," Charlie said. "I grew up in Astoria. I know what I'm talking about."

"And I suppose Italians never give revenge a second thought," said Ira.

Nina cut in. "Enough ethnic mudslinging. We'll stipulate that Angela looks like a scary broad. But there's one problem with the Angela theory. The murder must have been planned well in advance. It doesn't seem like it could have been done on the spur of the moment. How long had Angela known that Barry was cheating on her?"

"Well, everyone in this house knew," said Ira. "The Sunday before Barry died, there was a big discussion about it. Someone had spotted Barry and Jenny together down at the nude beach, causing major speculation."

"Did anyone tell Angela?" Nina asked.

"You're talking about Davis Park," Jonathan said. "Nobody has to tell anybody anything. Everyone just knows."

"So Angela could have heard about Jenny," Charlie said, "and stolen an unused patch from Barry's bedroom, returned to the city, poisoned it, and snuck it back into the box."

It didn't sound right to Nina. "Nah," she said. "I think Cheryl was right."

"About what?"

"It must have been someone who had hated Barry deeply

for a very long time. Not someone who was momentarily pissed off at him."

The thing of it was, Nina knew that the only person around who fit that description was Jonathan. She examined him in profile. The sensitive mouth, the sweet blond curls, the Lands' End wardrobe. She had known all along that it had been too good to be true. She wondered if anybody ever had the kind of life where things turned out to be too good to be false.

CHAPTER 27

The next day dawned bright. Well, not exactly bright, but brighter. There was still a cloud cover, but it was a thin, wispy layer of cirrus clouds, replacing the thick cumulus soup they'd been in all week. Cheryl took her coffee out on the deck. As she went, she gave Nina a small nod, the way a mob leader would gesture to one of his henchmen to follow him, or a dog trainer would signal an enrollee in obedience school. Nina followed, feeling more like a Labrador retriever puppy than a member of the Gambino crime family.

"What have you found out?" Cheryl asked, not exactly out of the side of her mouth, but almost.

"About what?" If Cheryl was going to treat her like a puppy, she was going to display the intelligence of one.

"About Jonathan." Half Gambino, half Red Queen, totally scary.

"What about him?" Nina was enjoying her puppy role and briefly considered licking Cheryl's face.

"Jesus Christ, stop acting like a moron. Did you find out if Jonathan gave Barry those things?"

"What things?"

"Those transdermal things. Those patches."

Suddenly Nina felt very conflicted. Well, that wasn't really accurate. There was nothing sudden about it. Nina had felt conflicted every day of her life since nursery school, when she had developed a crush on a little boy named David Glasser, who she knew even at the time was an asshole.

But right now Nina felt so conflicted that she didn't know what to say. Now, that was a bit unusual. She knew that Cheryl would get all excited if Nina told her that Cheryl's suspicions were right. That Jonathan had indeed bought the box of transdermal patches in Canada and given them to Barry. Nina could see it all now—Cheryl would narrow her eyes and throw her head back in triumph. "I told you so," she'd crow.

Nina didn't want to play out that scene. Not because she was protecting Jonathan. After all, he claimed that he had already told the police about this. But somehow she couldn't bear to watch Cheryl rip him apart in absentia. How had Nina gotten into this situation anyway? Cheryl had set the whole thing up. In retrospect, Nina could see that Cheryl had bullied her into coming out for the week, thrown her together with Jonathan, then planted seeds of suspicion in her mind and set her off to hunt down Jonathan. Not like a Labrador retriever puppy, but like a bloodhound.

Actually, what it reminded Nina of was an old record album cover, a copy of *My Fair Lady* that her family had owned thirty years ago. It was the original cast recording with Julie Andrews and Rex Harrison. There was a drawing of George Bernard Shaw, up in heaven with wings and a halo, acting as a puppeteer, pulling the strings on Henry Higgins. Who in turn was pulling the strings on Eliza Doolittle. There was a three-way manipulation going on here, with Cheryl acting as the chief string-puller and Nina as the middle woman and Jonathan as Eliza.

Although, she didn't really feel like she'd been prying anything out of him. Everything he told her, he'd already told the police. So it wasn't technically a breach of confidence to relay the information to Cheryl. But it felt like one. Nina knew that Jonathan would not pick Cheryl to confide in. He didn't like her. She had B.P. Bad personality.

Of course, Nina might well ask herself why, if Cheryl was the kind of person no one wanted to hang out with, Nina was spending so much of her time hanging out with her. What was it Jonathan had said about Barry? That he made Jonathan feel like he was living his life in color instead of black and white.

Did Nina feel that way about Cheryl? Not really, but there was something about Cheryl Schneiderman that Nina found exciting. What exactly? Probably the way that Cheryl said whatever she thought. While Nina overanalyzed, examined the implications, and struggled with her eternal ambivalence.

Nina used to feel that the presence of ambivalence was a sign of a higher form of life. She'd fostered it, tending to it as if it were a prickly but rare and valuable plant. Lately she had started to feel that ambivalence was present in everyone, but that successful, effectual people were able to beat it back. For the past few years, she had been engaged in a marathon wrestling match with her overdeveloped sense of ambivalence, which had grown huge and strong from all those years of tending, like a vegetable injected with colchicine.

It was something that Nina admired in Cheryl, who had reduced her sense of ambivalence to a ninety-eight-pound weakling who could be pinned to the mat in ten seconds flat. She was an inspiration, that woman.

Carried away with the concept, Nina made a quick decision to tell all. "Yeah, he gave them to Barry," she said. "He got them when he was in Canada last summer."

"And he admitted that to you? Just like that?"

"Uh-huh."

"I think we should go to the police with this," Cheryl said.

"He already told the police."

"How do you know?"

"He told me he told them."

"Just because he claims to have told the police doesn't mean he actually did."

"C'mon, Cheryl. Don't get carried away."

"Well, I for one am not going to get myself arrested for concealing evidence or being an accessory after the fact. We're going to call Detective What's-his-name right now and demand a meeting with him."

"Are you serious?" Nina didn't believe this.

"I'm dead serious."

"But how can you betray Jonathan like that?"

"Nina." Cheryl's voice and stare were level. "I'm going to the police with this. You can accompany me or not, whichever you prefer."

Jesus, look what Nina had started. Well, if she started it, she'd have to finish it too. "Okay, okay. I'll come with you, for Chrissakes."

"Good."

"I think that the detective's name is Ferrari. How do we do this?"

"I have his card," Cheryl said. "I kept it after he questioned me. I'll call him. But I'd like to meet with him somewhere we can have a little bit of privacy."

"Well, that leaves out this entire town. We could go to the Pines," Nina suggested hopefully. She had been there once, for an afternoon, years ago. It was definitely the prettiest place on Fire Island. The landscaping, the architecture, even the residents were more attractive than in neighboring towns. The natives made heterosexuals look like *shlubs*.

Nina had once read an interview with Larry Kramer, who had spent many summers out at the Pines. The interview disabused Nina of any notion she'd had that homosexual men had it easy in New York City. True, they didn't have to worry about their biological clocks or little mouths to feed. But, according to Kramer, they had the dual pressure of trying to be as successful as any heterosexual man and as beautiful as any heterosexual woman.

"No, not the Pines," Cheryl said. "It's too long a walk. And I don't feel like paying for a water taxi. We'll go over to Patchogue."

"Okay." Nina sounded meeker than she would have liked.

"And while we're there, we'll have him take us over to a shopping center. There are a couple of items I need."

"You're going to have a detective from Suffolk Homicide take you shopping?"

"Why not?"

"Cheryl, you're too much."

"I think I'm just enough, thank you very much."

At the moment, Cheryl's victorious battle over ambivalence seemed less than awe-inspiring. There was a lot to be said for self-doubt. Nina should never let herself forget that.

CHAPTER 28

Detective Ferrari was waiting to pick them up at the ferry in
Patchogue later that afternoon. He was young and cute. Not
cute in a way that made Nina clutch Cheryl by the arm and
whisper, "My God, is he cute." But cute in a way that you
only became aware of after a while. Like Bill Clinton, who
had seemed like a lowlife during the primary, but eventually
made even the classiest hearts flutter.

Nina remembered thinking, at first, Who does Clinton
think he's fooling, biting his lower lip in that mock humble
way? But now what was once irritating had become appealing. Whenever he was on the news, Nina hung around, hun-
grily hoping for a glimpse of his upper teeth.

Ferrari shared that same sexy mannerism. After he had
driven Cheryl and Nina over to a coffee shop in downtown
Patchogue and settled them into a booth, he leaned back and
grinned. "So," he said, and bit his lower lip.

"So," Cheryl said, and bit hers. It was a regular Arkansas standoff.

"Nice town," Nina said, to break the ice.

"It's okay," Ferrari said. "Patchogue's most famous native son is Jeffrey MacDonald."

"Who's that?"

"You know," Cheryl said with her contempt showing. "That doctor who killed his wife and kids in North Carolina. *Fatal Vision*."

Nina wasn't a true-crime fan, but she had seen the miniseries. "Oh, yeah. Did you know him?" she asked Ferrari.

"I'm not from around here," he said. "I grew up over in Lindenhurst and live in Coram now."

The waitress came over and asked if they needed menus.

"Just coffee for me, thanks," said Ferrari.

"Want to split a sandwich?" Cheryl asked Nina.

Of course Nina did not want to split a sandwich. If she had her druthers, she'd eat two. "Okay."

"Tuna on rye," Cheryl said. "And a diet Coke."

Tuna wasn't what Nina had in mind. But she absorbed the blow and went ahead and ordered a grapefruit juice. Someone in the house had guzzled all the citrus over the weekend and it had yet to be replaced. Nina was beginning to worry about scurvy.

Actually, Patchogue didn't seem like a particularly nice town. She never cared for those suburbs whose best feature was that they were as far away from the city as possible. Nina considered it a personal insult.

"So," Ferrari repeated, "you want to give me some help with the Adelman case. Is that the story?"

"Yes," said Cheryl, giving Nina a "let me handle this" kind of look. "Nina was talking to Jonathan Harris in a confidential manner and he told her that he bought a box of transdermal seasickness patches while he was in Canada last summer and gave them to Barry."

"Two boxes, actually," Nina said. "There are only two patches to a box."

The waitress brought their drinks and sandwich. Cheryl got to keep the plate, but let Nina have the pickle.

"Uh-huh." Ferrari seemed unimpressed. "What else did he tell you about the patches?" he asked Nina.

"That he assumed that the patch Barry used last Friday night was from the same supply—since they had only gone sailing once, and as far as he knew, Barry hadn't been on a boat at any other time."

"Well?" Cheryl was watching Ferrari like a hawk. Like a hawk with bad intentions.

"Well what?" The lip-biting standoff had been replaced by a glaring kind of standoff.

"Does that conform with what he told you?" Nina asked.

Ferrari nodded. "It does."

"So we haven't told you anything new?"

"Not really."

"Well, we're sorry if we wasted your time," Cheryl said, "but we thought it was important."

"It is. And don't worry about wasting my time."

"As long as we're here," Nina said, "could we ask you a few questions?"

"Sure."

"You know, we've been hearing so many rumors on the Island. We don't know what to believe. Could you tell us what kind of poison was used to kill Barry?"

"I can't give you the exact chemical composition. But I can tell you that it wasn't anything too sophisticated. Household ingredients were used, including nicotine, presumably from a pack of cigarettes. Perfect for transdermal application."

"So we're not looking for a Nobel prizewinning chemist here?" asked Nina.

"Nope. But we are looking for someone clever. It was cleverly done."

"That could be Jonathan," Cheryl said.

"That could be anyone," Ferrari added.

"I've been curious about one other thing," Nina said. "Did you find the box that the patches came in? And the individual wrapper that the patch Barry used came in?"

"Yeah." Ferrari was starting to sound cautious.

"Did the box have an expiration date on it?"

"Yeah."

"And did the wrapper?"

"Yeah."

"And did they match?"

Ferrari smiled. Then he bit his lower lip. "You're a clever one, aren't you?"

" 'Someone clever,' " Cheryl said. "Isn't that who we're looking for?"

Nina couldn't tell if Cheryl meant it or not. She said it in that tone of voice that mean people use when they want you to think they're only kidding, but you know there's more to it.

"Are you trying to tell me that the expiration dates on the box and the wrapper didn't match?" Nina asked.

"Look," said Ferrari. "I'm not at liberty to disclose the results of our investigation. Sorry."

"What does it mean, anyway?" Cheryl sounded furious. "Big deal, if the dates didn't match. Jonathan could still have gotten another box at another time, tampered with the patch, and made the switch."

"But," said Nina, "if the expiration date on the patch was later than the one on the box, whoever did it would have to have been in Canada recently." She was just thinking out loud. "Wouldn't you say so?"

"Hmmm." Ferrari made the syllable sound completely noncommittal.

"Yes." Cheryl was calming down. "I think you're right. It would have to have been someone who had visited Canada recently. Now, who could that be?"

Nina shrugged. "I have no idea."

"I think Elizabeth went to McGill undergrad. Maybe she's still got ties there." Cheryl gave Ferrari a helpful look as she polished off her half of the tuna sandwich.

"Please," said Nina, who had finished her half, plus their pickle, a while ago. "Elizabeth? It doesn't seem the least bit likely."

"Why don't you two leave the sleuthing to us?" Ferrari said. "But don't think I'm not grateful for the information you supplied us with."

"C'mon," Cheryl said, throwing some money down on the table. "We have a ferry to catch."

"I thought you wanted to go shopping." Nina fumbled with her wallet, intent on not owing Cheryl anything, but she was whisked away by the Red Queen before she could locate any singles.

CHAPTER 29

All the way back to the house, Cheryl acted weird. She snapped at Nina for nothing and her sentences wandered off in the middle. In general, she seemed irritable and distracted. Nina was relieved to get back to Davis Park, where Cheryl could spread her hostility among nine people instead of directing it all at Nina.

"Where have you two been?" asked Barbara, when they got back.

"Nowhere," Cheryl said.

"You're wearing shoes. Did you go over to Patchogue or something?"

"Maybe."

"For what?"

Cheryl mumbled a few hostile words and walked out of the house, letting the door slam behind her.

"What's wrong with her?" asked Barbara.

"What's always wrong with her?" countered Nina.

"Yeah."

"Actually, what *is* always wrong with her? I mean, what's the story? She's bad enough in the office, always telling everyone what they're doing wrong. But out here she's even more unbearable. I don't get it. What's her problem?"

"The usual." Barbara lowered her voice so that it wouldn't carry out to the deck. "Deprived of parental love as a child. Knocked around by the winds of fate, all that stuff."

"Look, we've all had less than ideal childhoods, I'm sure," said Nina. "But what turned Cheryl into such a dictator? There are very few people I would call genuinely nasty, but she would have to be one of them."

"Well, I heard something once that was kind of interesting. About her father."

"Her parents are divorced, right?"

"Yeah, for a long time," Barbara said. "Since she was in junior high school, I think. Anyway, when her parents split up, her father completely disappeared. And it wasn't until she was away at college that he reappeared."

"She went to Rutgers, didn't she?"

"Right. She once told me she wanted to go somewhere more Seven Sisterish, but her mother couldn't afford it. So she made her go to a state school."

"Sounds reasonable." Nina was of two minds on the subject. On the one hand, being a graduate of the State University of New York, she always got resentful when someone acted like going to a private college was a yet-unpublished addendum to the Bill of Rights. On the other hand, she did spend four years packed into huge lecture classes of three hundred students. It was easy to fall between the cracks. The cracks were so wide, it was hard to walk around them.

"I guess." Barbara clearly wasn't interested in the subject.

"She's an only child, isn't she?"

"Uh-huh."

"So what happened with her father?"

"Well, it sounded pretty weird the way I heard it. She was a freshman, living in the dorm at Rutgers, and hadn't seen her father in about five years. One day he shows up at her dorm room, unannounced, out of nowhere. After that, he started hanging around, dropping in at least once a week, sort of romancing her, if you know what I mean."

"Sounds sleazy."

"Just wait. Then he gets into the habit of taking her and her roommate out to dinner, buying them drinks and all. The next thing you know . . . ."

"Don't tell me," Nina said. "He seduces the roommate."

"Right."

"Well, it's better than seducing Cheryl, I guess."

"I guess. But Cheryl took it pretty badly, feeling violated and betrayed and all. I mean, if you think about it, the scenario has potential for an awful lot of Freudian subplots with age-old themes."

Nina agreed. "That's true. A father that disappears when you're thirteen could contribute heavily to a whopper of an Electra complex."

"Definitely."

"How did you find this out? Did Cheryl actually tell you all this?" Probably not, Nina thought. Cheryl Schneiderman was not quite the type to trot out her vulnerabilities for public display.

"Not exactly." Barbara looked embarrassed, but not very. "Actually, I heard it from somebody who used to be in Cheryl's therapy group."

"You're kidding." That was the problem with group therapy. There was no professional code of ethics for the members.

"No, it's true. A friend of my cousin's."

"So it was the opinion of your cousin's friend that this

traumatic event triggered the personality defects we observe in Cheryl Schneiderman today?"

"Well, you can imagine. Issues with trust, hostility toward men, all that stuff you can develop on your own, even without your father dragging your college roommate off to bed."

"Has she ever been in a stable relationship?" asked Nina. "As far as you know?"

"Stable?"

"Or something approaching stable." A pun came to mind about Cheryl being part of Barry's stable. But then Nina remembered that Barbara had been part of his stable as well, so she passed on the pun.

"You know that she was married once, don't you?" Barbara asked.

"I had no idea."

"Yeah, when she was very young. Her senior year of college."

Nina was always shocked when she heard that anyone she knew had gotten married in their early twenties. It just wasn't done, certainly not by the kind of people who ate at Ollie's Noodle Shop and bought their clothes at Eileen Fisher. "She never told me," Nina said.

"Me either. I heard it from my cousin's friend. She got married right around graduation to some guy in her class. They had both been accepted at the same law school. Syracuse, I think it was."

"That's right," Nina said. "Cheryl went to law school in Syracuse."

"So they got an apartment up there and started school together. By the end of the first year, they had broken up and he had dropped out."

"That's what marrying Cheryl Schneiderman will do to you."

"It was a disaster, according to my cousin's friend. She

had only done it to break loose of the erotic grip her father had on her."

"Very dramatic."

"Maybe I am being overly dramatic, but you get the idea."

"This is extremely interesting, I must say."

"Nina Fischman, I'd say that you're probably a sucker for this kind of thing."

"That's true. But this is a cut above the usual stuff. You know, all those depressed mothers struggling with their self-esteem and those remote fathers that played golf all weekend. The plots get stale."

"Yes, it's rare that you get to hear such a pronounced psychosexual theme in anyone's childhood story, isn't it?" Barbara asked.

"It is, and I suppose it's better to keep it that way." Nina liked her share of gossip. But she didn't go so far as to enjoy hearing about her friends starring in scripts that could be sold as movies of the week. "It's amazing I never knew any of this."

"Not if you think about it." Barbara got up and walked over to the refrigerator. She pulled out two beers and handed one to Nina. "I mean," she continued, "how much do you really know about her? Cheryl always makes herself heard, but never in an intimate way. I'm amazed she was ever even in a therapy group. It's not her style."

Barbara was right. Cheryl was both overbearing and remote at the same time. It made Nina wonder how much else she didn't know about her.

"Who are we gossiping about now?" Estelle asked, coming in from the deck.

"Cheryl," Nina answered. "Care for some?"

"Cheryl Schneiderman. Now, there's a topic that could

keep us going for the rest of the week." Estelle laughed with delight, but without any discernible meanness.

"I was telling Nina about her marriage. Did you know she had been married in her early twenties?" Barbara asked.

"I did."

"You did? Who did you find out from?"

"From Cheryl."

"No kidding."

"That's the thing about being a s-s-stutterer. It can go two ways. You either end up a very dominating s-speaker, holding on to the floor for dear life. Or, if you lack the requisite competitive edge, you retreat and become a good listener. And that way you get to find out all kinds of things from all kinds of people."

"Including Cheryl?"

"Es-s-specially Cheryl. She falls into the category of mistrusting people. Women like her are walking around with a pent-up need to s-spill their guts. S-so when s-someone like her comes up against s-someone like me, it's like she's arrived at the oracle of Delphi or s-something. She'd ask me what I thought of this or that and I'd s-silently shake my head yes or no, trying to imbue the atmosphere with incredible wisdom."

Barbara was not finding this amusing. She seemed competitive when she asked, "What else did you find out about her?"

"That she was in love with Barry Adelman."

"Really?" Barbara asked. "Even though he dumped her last summer?"

"He never really dumped her. They were s-still s-sleeping together, as a matter of fact."

"You know this for sure?"

"Absolutely. She s-saw him at least once a week all winter in the c-city."

"One thing puzzles me," Nina said. "How did this guy find the time for all these women?"

"You make it sound like it was a diverting little hobby," Barbara said. "It was an addiction. How does a drug addict find the time to embezzle or steal enough money to score enough dope to get him through the week?"

"Barbara's right. Barry never s-sat down with his weekly planner and penciled everyone in. He was driven: he ran from one to the next, propelled by sheer animal instinct coupled with the cunning of the addicted."

"But why did Cheryl put up with it?" Nina asked. "What kept her coming back for more? She must have known that there was nothing in it for her."

"There must have been an addiction on her s-side as well. From what she told me, it s-seems that she had tried many times to s-stop s-sleeping with him. But she was incapable."

"I guess the old Häagen-Dazs in the freezer analogy applies," said Nina.

"Yup. She couldn't s-stop herself. Cheryl just couldn't find a way to get rid of him."

That stopped everyone short. Barbara and Nina giggled nervously. "Interesting choice of words, don't you think?" asked Barbara.

"Hmmm." Estelle gave her an oracle of Delphi kind of nod.

CHAPTER 30

The house was quiet. Everyone was off at the Casino having a predinner drink and Nina thought it would be a good opportunity to take a nap. She hadn't been sleeping all that well lately.

For one thing, the walls were paper-thin and someone sneezing in the next room could wake you up. But the real problem was that Barry's murder had spooked her. Nina's confusion about Jonathan was contributing to her insomnia as well. Besides, she wasn't used to sharing her room with anyone. She thought back to the summer she traveled around Europe, staying in youth hostels that slept twelve to a room. Or cheap pensiones, when she even had to share a bed with a stranger at times. She didn't recall missing a night's sleep then. Nina supposed she was becoming a lower-middle-class version of "The Princess and the Pea."

Or maybe it was who she was sharing the room with. Estelle's words kept crowding into Nina's already overcrowded mind: *She couldn't find a way to get rid of him.* Nina had spent the week obsessing about whether or not Jonathan had killed Barry. Perhaps she should have shifted her attention to her roommate.

She surveyed the contents of the bedroom. Cheryl's belongings were minimal. There was a stack of towels and beach blankets on a shelf above the door. Hanging from the shelf was a wire basket that contained skimpy things—Cheryl's underwear and bathing suits. Most of her clothing was on hangers, hung on hooks sunk into the wooden walls.

Nina reached for the rayon jumpsuit she had borrowed for the jungle-theme party. Was it only last Friday? She felt the fabric, then stuck her hand into the pocket and pulled out a crumpled piece of paper. Nina sat down on her bed and smoothed the paper out against her knee. It had a phone number on it, just seven digits, no area code. She ran upstairs to the phone and dialed the number, just to see. A prerecorded message kicked in, giving the schedule for a Patchogue movie theater. Four different crummy movies were playing. So much for Nina's brilliant detecting instincts. She went back downstairs, recrumpled the paper, and returned it to the pocket of Cheryl's jumpsuit.

But once she had started she couldn't stop. Sleuthing was a more powerful urge than eating potato chips. Maybe even up there with those shrimp chips they give you in Thai restaurants. Now, Nina could go on all night with those.

She turned to the nightstand that stood between the two beds. Cheryl had a pile of paperback novels stacked up. There was nothing more telling, Nina felt, than a person's taste in literature. Some people might scrutinize another's hair or voice or shoes. But to Nina, what one read revealed far more than a pair of Ferragamo pumps.

She flipped through Cheryl's stack. It contained some very weird stuff. Weird to Nina, anyway, who mostly confined her reading to books by women or gay men born after Pearl Harbor who resided in a metropolitan area with a population that exceeded two million (May Sarton and Jane Austen being notable exceptions).

Cheryl's reading matter was written entirely by men. Judging by the covers, the books all belonged to some sort of technothriller genre that Nina had never previously encountered. There had to be something wrong with a thirty-seven-year-old woman who chose to read about groups of men blowing each other away with sophisticated weapons.

What did it mean? Nina had heard that all women had traces of male hormones in their system, some more than others. Was Cheryl suffering from testosterone poisoning? She was sort of flat-chested and her fat-to-muscle ratio was more reminiscent of Sylvester Stallone than Marilyn Monroe. So was her personality. Cheryl would be more likely to shoot someone's head off than fall into a suicidal victimesque state.

But why think so stereotypically? Nina scolded herself. Just because Cheryl had trained herself to be a scrappy street fighter didn't mean she had a biochemical imbalance.

Nina picked up one of the technothrillers. It fell open to a bookmarked page. The bookmark was a postcard, a reproduction of an art poster. It was a photograph of a sculpture, a large bronze of a couple sitting on a park bench. *"Banc des Amoureux,"* the caption read, followed by *"Jardin Botanique de Montréal."* Nina flipped the postcard over, where a few lines were scrawled in a feminine handwriting. *"Dear Cheryl,"* the card read, *"I trust that you got my package. If not, let me know. Regards to Mindy. Hope all is well. Love, Ruth."* The card had been postmarked in Montreal.

Jesus, a package from Canada. Nina's immediate instinct was to assume that the box that Ruth sent Cheryl contained motion-sickness patches. Which were available over-the-counter in Canada but not in the States. This was Nina's immediate instinct, but was it necessarily the truth?

Who was Ruth, anyway? And if Nina confronted her, would Ruth reveal the contents of the package she sent to Cheryl? She reached for Cheryl's purse, opened it, and fumbled around for an address book. But she came up empty.

Well, there were several approaches that Nina could take. She could wave the postcard in front of Cheryl's face and demand to be told exactly what was in the package. But that and a token would get her on the subway. Cheryl didn't seem like the type to burst into a teary confession.

Or she could somehow get in touch with Ruth, who might cave in and reveal all. Except that Nina didn't know Ruth's last name. According to the contents of the postcard, Ruth apparently knew Mindy. So Nina could ask Mindy how to get in touch with Ruth. But Nina didn't even know how to get in touch with Mindy.

Someone in the house might be able to help her. Who was it that said he had a crush on Mindy? Ira or Charlie? It was sometimes hard to tell those two apart. Nina was pretty sure it had been Charlie. She bet he would at least know Mindy's last name, if not her phone number. In Nina's experience, it was hard to remain ignorant of the surname of the object of your crush.

She'd ask Charlie if he knew how to reach Mindy and then ask Mindy how to reach Ruth. And then try cross-examining Ruth long-distance.

Or she could just call Detective Ferrari, read him the contents of the postcard, and forget the whole thing. But that wouldn't be nearly as interesting.

CHAPTER 31

That night at dinner, Nina waylaid Charlie on his way to the bathroom. "Psst," she hissed from the hallway, as if in a spy movie.

"What's up?" He had already begun to unzip his fly, since the toilet was within sight.

"I need to get in touch with Mindy. Do you have her phone number? Or at least her last name?"

"Of course I have her phone number. Hope springs eternal. What do you want to talk to her about? Did you decide that she murdered Barry after all?"

"Not exactly." Nina felt that familiar tug of temptation to tell all. Some people have instincts for privacy, for hoarding their thoughts. Nina was a sharer rather than a hoarder. Her first impulse was always to sit down, order a decaf, and start talking.

But it would clearly be a mistake in these close quarters.

Not that the house was a viper's nest, but it was, as she had discussed with Jonathan, a fishbowl.

"Then why?" Charlie's hands landed on his fly again and his eyes flickered toward the bathroom.

"Look, go take a leak. Then give me Mindy's number. And you'll find out everything in due time."

He did as he was told, and Nina slipped out in the middle of dinner, mumbling something about Jonathan expecting her. Once the excuse was used, she decided to take herself up on it and headed over to his house.

The occupants were sprawled all over the living room, while the remains of dinner were sprawled all over the screened-in porch. The house might feature several original works of sculpture, but they were obviously not known for K.P.

"Hello there." Jonathan jumped up from his seat and came over to give her a one-armed hug.

"I need to use your phone."

"What's the matter? Is yours out of order?"

"No, just inconveniently located." At this point, she became aware of the fact that the entire room was listening to their conversation. She looked at the phone sitting on the coffee table, a mere foot from three people's knees. "You wouldn't have an extension by any chance, would you?"

"No. Need some privacy?"

"It would be nice."

"I have an idea. Richie, can Nina use your phone?"

"Sure." Richie shrugged with the affability of a regular guy from Brooklyn.

"Richie's house is right next door. And he's alone out here this week. So we invited him for dinner. Richie, this is Nina."

"Hi." He reached over and gave her hand a squeeze.

"Hi. Thanks for the use of your phone. It's hard to have a private conversation around here."

"Tell me about it." Richie had a great smile. In comparison, Jonathan looked pale and overbred, devoid of the warmth of the boroughs. Then Nina noticed a pack of cigarettes in Richie's pocket and the image of desirability was dispelled.

Jonathan led her over to the house next door, which was humble but empty. The emptiness gave it an air of luxury. She could have been at Blenheim Palace instead of a plywood-paneled beach shack with nylon plaid upholstered furniture.

"I suppose you want to know what's going on," she said.

"If you want to tell me."

"Thanks for not asking. But I'll tell you. I've got to tell somebody. I've always got to tell somebody."

"Okay."

"What I'm trying to do is absolve you of the murder of Barry Adelman."

"Well, ma'am, I'd be much obliged."

He was so cute. What had she been thinking of with Richie? "But first I need some more information." She explained about the postcard and Mindy and Ruth. "What do you think?"

"Good theory," he said. "But what's Cheryl's motive? I always thought she was a little unhinged, but why should her madness go in the direction of killing Barry?"

Nina recounted her conversation with Barbara about Cheryl's past. And Estelle's revelation about Cheryl's sexual addiction to Barry. "Enough motivation for you?" she asked.

"I don't know. I mean, we've all got stories. But I personally have never murdered anyone. Have you?"

"Not yet. But people do. You've read all those newspaper accounts—the neighbors can't believe that good old Mac next door could have done it. He seemed like such a nice, regular guy. Yet there's his wife, all hacked to bits, and Mac's prints are all over the ax."

"I don't know." Jonathan sat down on the couch and put his feet up on the coffee table.

"Look, somebody did it. Probably somebody you know. Does anyone seem like a likely suspect?"

"I guess not. But what's your plan? How are you going to get Mindy to give you Ruth's phone number? And how are you going to get Ruth to tell you what was in the package?"

"The first part is easy. I'll just say that Cheryl went somewhere and asked me to call Ruth while she was gone and I lost the number."

"Where could Cheryl have gone so that she couldn't call Ruth herself? It doesn't make sense."

"Oh, I don't know. On a boat. On your boat. I'll tell her that you're having this whirlwind romance with Cheryl and the two of you went off on your sailboat and can't be reached."

"Mindy would never believe it. She knows that I'm not Cheryl's type."

"Okay. But that gives me an idea. Let me think about this for a minute."

"All right. Sit down next to me." Jonathan patted the couch.

Nina snuggled in at his side. "How about this?" she said. "Ruth doesn't know you, does she?"

"I've never even heard of her."

"Well, we tell Ruth that you and Cheryl are a hot item and you're both off on your boat. Meanwhile, Cheryl asked me to call Ruth and tell her to send more of those transdermal patches that she sent before. Cheryl needs them because she's been spending so much time on your boat. If Ruth denies sending them, she's either telling the truth or covering for Cheryl. But there's a chance that she did send them to Cheryl without knowing what she wanted them for. In that case, she just might admit freely to the whole thing."

"It might work."

"Okay. Let's see if we get anywhere with Mindy first." Nina dialed the number that Charlie had given her. Mindy picked up on the first ring.

"Hello?" Her voice had a throaty quality often found in women of Nassau County origin. Nina had always wondered about this. An ENT doctor had once told her that the syndrome was due to vocal polyps, developed during overuse.

"Hi. Mindy?"

"Yes?"

"This is Nina Fischman, a friend of Cheryl Schneiderman's."

"Oh, yeah. I know who you are. You work with her, am I right?"

"That's right."

"And you took my place in the house."

"Yes, I'm out here right now, as a matter of fact."

"How is it out there?"

"Rainy." Nina steered clear of the topic of Barry Adelman's death. "There's something I need your help with."

"What's that?"

"Cheryl asked me to call her friend Ruth and gave me the number. But now I can't find it and Cheryl's not around. I thought you might have it. Cheryl mentioned to me that you knew her."

There was at least fifteen seconds of silence on the other end of the line. Nina waited it out. She had decided it was better not to start making up stories about where Cheryl was or why she asked Nina to call Ruth unless Mindy asked her for a specific explanation.

"That's bullshit, isn't it?" Mindy finally said.

"Excuse me?"

"That's bullshit about Cheryl asking you to call Ruth, isn't it?"

"Hmmm?" It was the most neutral thing Nina could think to say.

"This is about Barry, isn't it?"

"Well, I, ummm . . ."

"Look, if you want to talk about this, maybe we should talk about it in person. When are you coming back to the city?"

"I don't know. But if there's something you really think is worth discussing, I could come in anytime."

"This is definitely worth discussing. If you're trying to figure out who murdered Barry, that is. Which is what I think you're trying to do."

"Boy," Nina said. "That didn't take you long. I hardly got one sentence out."

"Well, I've been waiting to have this conversation. I'm just surprised no one called me sooner."

"Can I meet you for lunch tomorrow?" Nina asked.

"Lunch is good. I work near Grand Central. Meet me at the information booth at twelve-thirty. Is that okay?"

"Sure."

"And," Mindy warned throatily, "don't mention anything to Cheryl."

CHAPTER 32

Jonathan had offered to go with her, but it didn't seem like a good idea. Nina kept very quiet about her departure, slipping out of the house before anyone was up and catching the first ferry.

The train out of Patchogue was filled with commuters. It had always seemed extraordinary that people actually spent three and a half hours a day in a railroad car, but Nina could sort of see it now. It wasn't a railroad car so much as a big clubhouse on wheels. People seemed to have their regular seats, their regular seatmates, and their regular card games. Nina could hardly concentrate on her magazine for the racket that went on around her. It was like being in her junior high school lunchroom. The only thing missing was the spitballs.

Nina sat alone, quietly by the window, as she had in junior high school, and watched Suffolk and then Nassau counties pass by. Long Island seemed past its prime. Once a glorious empire carved out of potato fields, now the strip shopping centers and town sumps spoke of faded glory, the promised land no more. The pioneers who had bravely purchased cars and houses and headed east from Brooklyn and Queens were now battling cancers—breast, prostate, and skin. Perhaps the skin cancer was from all those weekends taking the kids to Jones Beach.

But why was the breast cancer rate so alarmingly high in Nassau County? Nina had heard tales of overcrowded waiting rooms at North Shore Oncology, of staggering statistics. Was it the water supply, the genetic composition of the indigenous stock, the high-fat diet consumed at the steak houses that still lined Jericho Turnpike? No one knew. Well, this was one case where being too paralyzed to leave the Bronx had paid off for the Fischman family, even if Nina did have to dodge more than just spitballs back in junior high school.

Penn Station was a hot and muggy nightmare and Nina got out of there as soon as she could. Grand Central was sure to be cooler and classier. The Westchester commuters had smaller hair and finer bones. But Nina had a couple of hours to kill before she met Mindy, so she decided to go home and empty her mailbox.

The Thirty-fourth Street IRT station always presented a quandary. It was the only station Nina used that had separate platforms for the local and express trains. So if you were headed for a stop like Seventy-second Street, as Nina was, you had to walk down and up an extra stairway if you wanted to catch the express and save two and a half minutes. But the express usually pulled in and out while you were still on the stairs, effectively ruining your time gain. Nina tended to opt for the local. It was indulgent, she knew, but as a professional woman she felt she had earned a bit of luxury in her life.

The train came and she got uptown without incident. Emergency-cord pulling had become almost epidemic on the

Broadway local. What kind of sociopath would get joy out of pulling an emergency cord on a subway train? Nina wondered. Graffiti she could understand, turnstile jumping, door holding, riding between cars were all activities that held some sort of adventure. But it took a truly sick mind to pull a cord. It was a crime against humanity.

She couldn't really complain about the subway, however. Nina was of a generation that was still thrilled to find that the air-conditioning was working. She remembered those long commutes in the summers when she was home from college, living in her parents' East Bronx apartment, sweating as the White Plains Road train slowly wound its way downtown, taking her to whatever crummy job she had managed to dig up for the season. Air-conditioned subway cars were still unheard of at the time, even on the IND—which at that time was the state-of-the-art subway line.

She exited the train to a broiling subway platform and got on line for the stairway. The Seventy-second Street station had gotten a little less crowded due to recent renovations, but it still seemed jammed no matter what time of day it was.

The intersection of Seventy-second and Broadway was as architecturally unremarkable as ever, yet it always made Nina's heart pound. The people hurriedly trying to make it across Broadway before the light changed—it was a particularly wide intersection—were certainly not superb physical specimens. They were, for the most part, short and dark and squat and worried-looking. But they looked smart, and that was enough to make Nina keep the Ansonia Station as her post office forever.

She cut down a side street and entered her lobby. Her mailbox was practically empty. Her neighbor must have checked it. She headed up the shabby stairway. In the patchwork gentrification that had hit the Upper West Side, Nina's building stood as a testament to the old times, the days of white flight and rooming houses. Not that the tenants in her building were poor. Many had prospered, but were addicted to their below-market rents.

Brian and Arthur, for example, the gay couple who shared the fourth floor with her. Arthur had still been a medical student when he first moved in. He was a psychiatrist now, with a healthy-enough practice. Yet he and Brian stayed in their small rent-stabilized apartment, while they poured money into their country home.

They had bought a weekend house in Columbia County. She had been up there once to visit. They had an odd thing going. Their house was a nineteenth-century row house within walking distance of the train station in Hudson. Every Friday night, they'd stock up at Fairway on cheese and pasta, catch a train, and carry their shopping bags over to their superbly restored town house. Which wasn't really a town house but a country house. At one tenth the price it would have been in the Village. And they spent the weekends doing exactly what they'd do if they were on Barrow Street—antiquing, stripping wood, and throwing dinner parties. And they didn't even own a car.

Brian, the younger of the two, heard her coming up the stairs and popped his head out. "I emptied your mailbox for you, even though you didn't ask me to. I noticed that everything was all crammed in there." They kept each other's keys.

"Thanks. I forgot to tell you I'd be away." The truth was that Nina never cared much about getting her mail. It was either junk or bills. And the bills, if lost, would come again.

"Where have you been?"

"Fire Island. Davis Park."

"Couldn't last the week?"

"I'm going back out this afternoon. I just had to come in to town for an appointment. Want to come in?"

"I'll be over in a minute. Just let me save my document and I'll bring you your mail." Brian was a writer. Before noon, he permitted himself to work on his novel. After that, he forced himself to turn his attention to the freelance articles he made his money from. He specialized in a variety of topics, including dog grooming and South American travel.

Nina let herself into her apartment and turned on the answering machine. Her friend Carol's voice came on. "I know you're away, but I thought you might beep your machine." She might, if she could ever find her beeper again. "So if you get this message before Tuesday, call me, because I have TDF vouchers for *The Sisters Rosensweig*. But I have to send them in by Tuesday, so let me know if you're interested."

Oh, well, too late. She'd have to wait until it appeared on the TKTS board. Which would be a while, since it was a sellout. Wendy Wasserstein's popularity always surprised Nina. How ironic that people found the woman so fascinating that they'd stand in line to pay sixty dollars to see her plays but no one wanted to be her. Nina knew this for a fact because she had taken a poll to see whether people would rather be Wendy or her investment banker brother. Wendy lost big. Nina took the poll again after Wendy's Pulitzer and Bruce still won.

Nina checked the rest of the messages. Nothing from Tom. The doorbell rang and she let Brian in. He handed her a pile of mail and picked out a postcard. "Tom's having a good time," he said. "Are you?"

She took a look at the card. It was from the Adirondack Museum near Indian Lake. *"Annie's showing great promise as a camper and canoer,"* she read. *"And the weather's been spectacular. See you soon. XXX Tom."*

"What's with the XXX?" she snapped at Brian. "What does XXX actually mean?"

"It doesn't mean anything. It's purely an evasionary tac-
tic to get around the *L* word. Who's Annie?"

"His daughter."

"Well, that's okay then."

"Yeah, just great. Brian, I'm never going to get married."

"Me either."

"Look, I'm sure that coming to terms with your homo-
sexuality, when you were sixteen years old and living in some
farming community in Wisconsin, was no picnic. But at least
you made peace with it. You know your outcome. This being
unmarried and almost forty makes me so jumpy. I'm constantly trying to guess how this play is going to end. Mrs.
Susan told me I was going to have two children. Where are
they?"

"Who is Mrs. Susan?"

"A fortune-teller who used to have a storefront on Sheri-
dan Square."

"I see."

"This was in the seventies, before astrology became a Republican thing."

"I've got to get back to my article," Brian said. "Dining
alfresco in Bahia."

"How did the German shorthaired pointer piece come
out?"

"Good. I'll show you the proofs." He turned to leave.

"Brian, I'm sorry if I sound like a whiny spoiled brat. I
know that many of your friends are fighting for their lives
and here I am complaining about some man because he
won't write *love* on a postcard."

"Don't be silly, Nina. You should have heard them before
they started fighting for their lives. When it came to whining,
they would have made you sound like St. Francis of Assisi."
Brian let himself out.

CHAPTER 33

Mindy was instantly recognizable. She was a tall Jewish blonde, made blonder—as most Jewish blondes are—by chemical intervention. She wore the Jewish-blonde expression of self-satisfaction, a "Why did God choose me?" look on her face.

Nina waved and strode right over to her. "I'm Nina Fischman." She extended her hand.

Mindy took it. "Oh, hi. I realized after we got off the phone that we forgot to describe ourselves. I was worried about recognizing you."

"Yeah, I know." Nina had never not recognized someone, even without a description. It was one of her talents, along with figuring out people's middle names—initials helped, but she did have a talent.

"How did you know it was me?" Mindy asked.

"Charlie described you."

"Oh, Charlie." Mindy's smile was a wistful one that wondered why she couldn't ever fall for the nice guys, only the shitheads. But mixed in with the wistfulness was a bitchy "I wouldn't be caught dead with him" look. "How is Charlie?"

"Fine. As fine as any of us are out there. Considering what happened to Barry."

"Yeah. Well, where shall we eat?"

Mindy looked like a major league salad head. The only thing you could do with people like that was suggest sushi. It wasn't something Nina craved very often, but it was a good excuse to drink beer. "Is there a decent sushi place around here?" Nina asked.

"Sushi. Good idea. We can go to Hatsuhana on Forty-eighth Street. It's a little pricey, but at least you know that it's fresh."

"Okay." Nina supposed that twenty-something dollars was a small price to pay for any information that Mindy might have. Besides, she always got a kick out of walking into a midtown Japanese restaurant with another woman. They were such male domains, it was like giving them the finger. Even if she was accompanied by a South Shore JAP who probably sniffed every handroll before she bit into it.

As they cut through the MetLife building, they made small talk about the rainy weather and the beach erosion on Fire Island. And Mindy talked a bit about her job. She worked as a headhunter specializing in the advertising industry. But neither of them said a word about Barry Adelman. When they were finally seated and Mindy had been talked into ordering a Kirin instead of Evian, Nina tried to seize the reins of the conversation.

"I think we have something important to talk about," Nina said. "About Barry. And Cheryl. And Ruth."

"I know." Mindy was still scanning the menu.

"I'm just getting the assorted sushi," Nina said. "It's too much trouble deciding on anything else."

"But that's like ordering the house wine."

"I always order the house wine. Not that I don't consider myself a thoughtful person. But I like to expend my energies elsewhere." It was Nina's private opinion that most women had menu disorders. She had seen the best of them waffling and grappling for far longer than was appropriate. And it seemed to get worse with age. Her own mother, a normally rational woman, could dissolve into a puddle of helpless indecision when faced with even the simplest coffee shop menu. What really annoyed Nina was these women's tendency to narrate their indecision. At least Cheryl had gone straight for a tuna fish sandwich, even if she was—perhaps—a murderer.

Mindy did about three minutes of menu narration before she settled on tuna sashimi. After all that.

Nina bit back her annoyance and launched in again. "When we spoke on the phone, it seemed that there was something you wanted to tell me. Something to do with Barry's murder."

"Okay, okay." Mindy took a sip of her Kirin beer. "This is good," she said.

"Isn't it?" Mindy couldn't be that bad. A Jewish woman who could appreciate beer was a rare thing.

"Okay. Here's the story. I've already talked to the police. But that was days ago, before I put two and two together. And once I figured the whole thing out, I knew I should call that detective back. But I just haven't been able to force myself to. . . ." She trailed off.

"And then I called," Nina prompted.

"And then you called, and I thought since you know Cheryl pretty well, you might be a good person to talk to. To help me figure out what to do."

"I'd like to help you very much. But first you have to fill me in."

"Right." Mindy fell silent again.

"Who's Ruth?"

"Ruth is this crazy friend of Cheryl's. I mean, I don't know if she's crazier than Cheryl. But she's sort of a character. Ruth and Cheryl grew up together in New Jersey."

"And now she lives in Montreal?"

"Yeah." If Mindy had been really sharp, she would immediately have asked Nina how she knew that. But it was hard to be naturally suspicious when you were brought up in Cedarhurst or Woodmere or Lawrence. "She married this French-Canadian guy she met in the Yucatán a couple of years ago. It didn't work out and I think they're divorced now, but she stayed up there. She says she likes it."

"Well, it's a pretty cool city."

"Is it?" Mindy asked. "I've never been there. Well, just for Expo, but I was a kid."

"It's great. As clean and beautiful as anyplace. But the people are like New Yorkers—they're dark and they walk fast and talk loud. It's the best of both worlds."

"Really? Well, as I said, Ruth is kind of a nut. But very friendly. She always wants to have dinner whenever she's in town to see her family. She also has a big mouth. Which is what started all of this."

"All of what?"

"Just listen, okay? I'll get there. This was my first summer in the house. Cheryl acted sort of weird about inviting me to take a share. I knew it was about Barry. She warned me about his womanizing, but I could tell that she still had a thing for him."

"According to Estelle, she never stopped sleeping with him," Nina said.

"I believe it. She watched him like a hawk. The whole time I was seeing him, I felt like I was under surveillance. She had a real love/hate thing with him. When he dumped me, I think it gave her some satisfaction. Which is part of the reason I dropped out of the house. Although I also think she felt sorry for me. She's not a monster or anything. Cheryl's complicated, you know."

"I know."

The sushi and sashimi arrived. Mindy delicately mixed her wasabi into her soy sauce like a maven. Nina layered a slice of ginger onto a slice of tuna roll and downed it in one gulp. She loved pickled ginger and often had to ask for seconds.

"Anyway," Mindy continued. "One weekend last month, when I was out at the house, the phone rang and I picked it up. It was Ruth. Cheryl wasn't around, so we chatted for a while. She said she was calling to make sure that Cheryl got the package she sent her. I said I didn't know. Then she asked me not to even tell Cheryl that she had called, since she wasn't supposed to mention the package to anyone. I said okay, and didn't think anything else about it. Until Detective Ferrari came to see me."

"Was that how you found out about Barry's death?"

"Yeah. Charlie called to tell me, but not until the day after the police contacted me."

"Charlie likes you," Nina said.

"I know. I think he called just to let me know that the competition was dead."

"He's a nice guy."

"Yeah, but I just don't want to settle." Mindy wrinkled her nose.

Those had been Charlie's exact words. Nobody wanted to settle. The world of dating was like one big litigation where neither side even wanted to negotiate, much less settle. A hopeless situation.

"Anyway," Mindy went on, "this cop comes by my office and starts asking me all these questions. Including when was the last time I'd been to Canada. Which I hadn't since col-

lege. I went to school in Buffalo and we used to go to Toronto
for Chinese food. I told him that, but it did make me think of
Ruth and wonder what she had sent Cheryl. But I didn't say
anything to him at the time."

"And then?"

"Charlie called the next day and told me about the motion-sickness patches and how they were from Canada. And
then I figured that they must have been what Ruth sent
Cheryl from Montreal. And that Cheryl must have tampered
with them and killed Barry."

"But you didn't call the police."

"No, I didn't know what to do. For one thing, Cheryl's a
friend of mine. For another, I'm scared of her."

"You think she's capable of doing something like that?"

"I know she is."

"How can you be sure?"

"There's one thing I haven't told you. Cheryl had a box
of patches from Canada. I saw them in her purse. I know I
shouldn't have gone through her pocketbook like that, but I
was desperate for a Tampax and there were none in the
house. Cheryl's purse was lying around our room and I rum-
maged through it. There weren't any Tampax, but there was
this box. It was a small box, but I picked it up because I
thought it might be some of those little tampons without ap-
plicators or something. And I know that it was from Canada
because on one side, the writing was all in French. I remember distinctly that it said *prévient le mal des transports*. And I
thought, 'Oh, now I know how to say "motion sickness" in
French.' So I couldn't really be mistaken, could I?"

"I would think not."

"So what do we do now?" Mindy asked.

"Good question."

"We could have one of those interventions. Like when a

friend of yours is all strung out on drugs. Everyone sits in a room and forces him to confront his problem."

"Think that would work with Cheryl? I don't," Nina said. "I mean, we're not asking her to check into Betty Ford for a couple of months. We're asking her to give herself up to a potential life sentence in prison."

"Maybe I should just call Detective Ferrari and tell him everything." Mindy played with her last slice of raw tuna and signaled for the check.

"That's probably best. You know, all this week, my number one suspect was Jonathan."

"Jonathan Harris? That's ridiculous. He's such a nice person. Actually, now that you mention it, Cheryl said something to me about him. And you."

"About Jonathan and me? What did she say?"

"It was after the Barry debacle, when I told her I was dropping out of the house. She said she'd try to find a replacement. And I said that whatever she did, she shouldn't find someone new to feed to Barry. And she said you would be perfect because you were one of the few people who would more likely be interested in Jonathan Harris than Barry Adelman. Then she gave this cackly kind of laugh, like Margaret Hamilton in *The Wizard of Oz.*"

"Funny, I usually think of her as the Red Queen."

"Anyway, she sort of cackled and said, 'That's what I'll do. I'll wind her up and set her off on Jonathan's trail.' "

"Which is what she did." Nina saw it all clearly now. And she felt like a *putz.* Cheryl knew that Jonathan would make a perfect murder suspect. She knew that he spent a lot of time in Canada and probably also knew that he kept Barry in Canadian transdermal patches. And if he wouldn't tell those things to the police, he might tell them to the pale, fuzzy, chubby soulmate that Cheryl had dragged out there for him. Nina Fischman. A perfect fall guy.

"I've got to get back." Mindy picked up the check. "Twenty-seven each, including the tip."

"Jesus, for three ounces of fish? That's like a hundred and fifty dollars a pound. This stuff is as expensive as a controlled substance."

"But at least it's fresh."

"Are you going to call Ferrari or should I?"

"No, I'll do it," Mindy said. "If she comes after me, she comes after me. Are you going back out there this afternoon?"

"You know, I think not." Nina weighed the pros and cons. "As a matter of fact, I think I could do quite nicely without ever going out there again."

CHAPTER 34

Nina walked over to Madison and then headed uptown.
There was something about Madison Avenue that always
proved calming. It was a world where affluent New Yorkers
still drank gin and bought leather goods, like in old movies.
Everyone was white and thin and had just gotten their clothes
pressed. Madison was untainted by people like Nina, who re-
fused to diet and needed a haircut. That was the fun of it,
walking on a street where you really didn't exist. Or if you
did, it was as a foreigner. It was relaxing to be out of the
mainstream, like being a tourist.

Nina's normally brisk gait would slow and she'd stare in
the shop windows at things she had never even been in a
room with—silver tea sets and bed linens that were actually
made out of linen.

As she turned left on Seventy-second and entered Central
Park, she began to wonder about Mindy. Nina had believed
what she said, had found her credible. But could she have

been setting Cheryl up? Could Mindy have killed Barry in a post–having-been-dumped rage? Maybe she had concocted the whole story.

By the time Nina had passed the Bethesda Fountain, she knew she had to go back out to Davis Park. She couldn't bow out now, with all these loose ends waiting to be tied up. Even for a person like Nina, who preferred character to plot, who could walk out on a movie five minutes before the end.

Mindy could be lying. And if she wasn't, Cheryl might have a reasonable explanation for why there had been a package of transdermal patches of Canadian origin in her purse. Although it was awfully hard to imagine what such a reasonable explanation might be.

As soon as Nina hit Central Park West, she stopped at a phone booth to give Brian a call. His machine clicked in. After the beep, she yelled into the phone, "It's Nina. Pick up if you're there."

"Howdy, neighbor," Brian drawled. "What can I do for you?"

"I've got to go back out to Fire Island and I don't know how long I'll be there. Could you do me a favor? Check my mail and my phone messages. And call me if anything important comes up. I'll give you my number."

"What does important mean?"

"Use your judgment. If I win the Publishers Clearing House Sweepstakes, please let me know."

"What's in it for me?"

"I'll buy you a car."

"What kind?"

"Either a Ford Escort or a Corvette. Depending on what the prize money is."

"In that case, I'll only call you if the jackpot is at least ten million. Okay?"

"That's fine, Brian." She dug around in her purse for the

number of the house in Davis Park. When she found it, she read it to him.

"Okay," he said. "I'll let you know if you get any important messages. From Publishers Clearing House. Or Tom."

"They both seem about as likely."

"Now, now, Nina. Bad attitude."

"I don't know how much I even care anymore." She felt herself going into a long-playing whine. Fortunately, the operator cut her off. Her three minutes were up. If she wished to continue whining, she had to deposit another nickel. Nina decided that it wasn't worth it. "I'll give you a call if I'm not back by Sunday."

"Okay. Have a good time."

Hardly, she thought.

CHAPTER 35

The next train to Patchogue wasn't until 5:07, so Nina took her time drifting downtown toward Penn Station. She stopped at the Coliseum Bookstore and almost bought a hardcover. Then she remembered the twenty-seven dollars she had spent on lunch and reconsidered.

It was ridiculous, she knew, to spend all that money on a few bites of uncooked fish and cramp up when it came to parting with a twenty for a week's worth of recreation. But she led a life where she had to make a choice between sushi and fiction and she was already in for the lunch. She pictured an existence where she could casually order the sushi deluxe platter and then spend the afternoon browsing and choosing among this season's crop of hardcovers. Or even trade paperbacks. But Nina seemed to be permanently stuck in a mass market income bracket. So she settled on last year's Anne Tyler and continued down Broadway.

She got momentarily distracted in Macy's Cellar, looking

at exotic condiments, and thought she might miss her train. But she inserted herself into a surge of sweaty commuters and ran down the stairs toward track nineteen in time to get a seat next to the window.

When the train pulled into Patchogue, she wavered between a walk and a cab to the ferry. She ended up taking a cab. Not because she was in a tremendous hurry, but because walking in the suburbs always proved highly unsatisfactory. All those German shepherds barking at you, some chained, some unchained. Nina was fond of canines, as long as they were fluffy and friendly. She didn't care for the pointy-snouted variety with moles on their cheeks, more dingo than dog.

The cab stunk of tobacco, and she was glad to get out and onto the ferry. But as soon as she sat down on the top deck, she started to worry. It would be clear from her shoes and purse and sedate outfit (a long, floral print skirt had replaced her boxer shorts) that she'd been in the city. She was sure to be cross-examined by Cheryl, if not the entire house. And Nina had no idea how to handle this. She could lie and say that she had an emergency doctor's appointment or felt like she needed to see her shrink. But she'd seen Cheryl cross-examine clients. Talk about dingoes! Nina would have preferred to avoid ending her days as a bloody carcass.

She hadn't really formulated a plan by the time she returned to the house. Cheryl was waiting on the front deck. "Welcome back." She sounded at her scariest. "Do you mind if we have a little chat?"

"Here?"

"Anywhere. Let's go down to the beach. It stopped raining for once."

"Okay." Okay was really all you could say to Cheryl most of the time. Even if you thought you were running the risk of being strangled to death by her on a deserted beach. "Let me

just dump my pocketbook and shoes." Hauling around a
Coach tote didn't quite make for carefree beach strolling.
Nina had a feeling that wasn't the point of this chat, but you
never knew when you might have to make a quick getaway.

"Hurry up."

"Okay, okay."

Cheryl was ominously silent on the boardwalk and by the
time they got to the beach, Nina was wound tight. The first
glimpse of the shoreline reassured her, however, since the
beach was far from deserted. It was filled with shareholders
who had been cooped up in overcrowded houses for too
many interminable rainy days. They were busy depleting
their surplus of stored glycogen—jogging, walking, tossing
Frisbees, and playing kadima.

Despite the foreign-sounding name, kadima was simply a
reworked version of paddleball, a game played by Bronx residents thirty years ago at the Shorehaven Beach Club, pres-
ently the site of a large cluster of modular steel housing. The
Fischman family had never joined Shorehaven. It had been
racially segregated, which seemed to bother no one other
than the Fischmans. Besides, Ida Fischman had a thing about
women who played mah-jongg. Therefore, Nina had inherited a thing about children who played paddleball.

She continued to avoid kadima. Somehow she felt politi-
cally justified. Anyway, she had a suspicion that it wasn't a
game at which she would excel. Her eye-hand coordination
was probably down in the lower percentiles. Her ear-mouth
coordination, however, was off the charts and she would need
every bit of it to get through this verbal duel with Cheryl.

By the time she had rolled up her skirt and stuck her toes
in the water, Nina was extremely nervous. A sudden urge to
avoid overcame her and she launched into a hastily constructed story about having to run back to the city on a moment's notice to help her mother, who was scheduled to have

some complicated medical procedure performed on her that day.

"It's something they do instead of a GI series, to see if you have an ulcer. They give you this tiny camera attached to a wire, and you swallow it. Then they pull it back up, getting close-ups of your upper gastrointestinal tract." Nina wasn't making the whole thing up completely; her mother had had such a test about a year ago.

"Nina, enough." Cheryl was on the high end of the Red Queen spectrum. "You don't have to make up any more of this bullshit. I talked to Mindy about an hour ago. We had a very interesting and revealing conversation."

"You did? Did she call you?"

"I called her."

"How come?"

"When it became clear that you had run away from home this morning, I had to sit down and talk with everyone in the house to find out where you went. Because I had a very uneasy feeling that wherever you were, it might have something to do with me."

"But I didn't tell anyone in the house where I was going." But I did tell Jonathan, Nina thought. Had he turned state's evidence?

"I was able to figure it out."

"How did you do that?"

"Charlie told me that you were fishing around for Mindy's phone number yesterday."

"He did?"

"Well, I practically terrorized the poor man."

"I can imagine."

"Yes, well, it seemed likely that your phone call to Mindy was connected to your disappearance. It didn't take a genius."

"And what did Mindy tell you?"

"That she ordered tuna sashimi and you ordered the mixed sushi platter. Nina, that doesn't show much imagination. If you find ordering Japanese food intimidating, maybe you should consider taking a course at the New School."

"What else did she tell you?" Nina steeled herself.

"Oh, just about everything. That you called her with some cock-and-bull story about needing to reach Ruth. And that you came rushing into town and she spilled her guts to you. That she told you about finding the patches in my pocketbook. And so on."

"Really? Jesus Christ, you must have interrogated her pretty thoroughly."

"I have my methods. I haven't spent ten years in Housing Court for nothing."

Indeed. Cheryl carried Housing Court around with her. She was like a hermit crab who had adopted the place as her permanent home and now dragged it wherever she went for shelter and protection.

"And by the way," Cheryl said. "In case you're wondering, she already called Detective Ferrari. He's probably on his way out here at this very moment."

"Oh." They walked a bit in silence.

It was the best time of the day. The sun was heading behind the dunes and a breeze was dispersing the heat. Clusters of people lay on blankets and sat in sand chairs, sharing pitchers of margaritas and iced tea.

Suddenly Cheryl clutched Nina's arm. Hard. "How could you?" she shrieked.

What choice did I have, thought Nina. But she remained silent.

"Where do your allegiances lie, for Chrissakes?" Cheryl kept hold of Nina's arm and continued to scream. "I was only doing what every other woman in this town wanted to do, but didn't have the courage to do. I did it for all of us."

"But Cheryl, really—"

"He was a menace. It was justifiable homicide. You see that, don't you?"

"It was a rather extreme solution," Nina said.

"Oh, God, I'm sick to death of all that conciliatory crap. These men, they fuck us over, time and again, and while we're sitting there, fantasizing about assassinating them, we're smiling and stroking them at the same time. What the hell is wrong with all of us?"

"What's wrong with you?" Nina said. "Barry was a sicko. Why did you continue to play into it, hanging around him, sleeping with him? You could have just walked away, letting him have Davis Park. Jesus, you live in New York City. You never would have had to see him again. You didn't have to kill him; you just had to ignore him."

"Ignoring things is not what I do best," Cheryl said. Her voice was shaky. Nina thought she might be getting ready to cry. But Cheryl took a deep breath and exhaled slowly, re-aligning her spine and tucking her pelvis under. Years of exercise classes had a permanent effect on Nina's generation of women: On the verge of being arrested for homicide? Watch your breathing and your posture and everything will be all right.

Tucking her pelvis under did seem to help, because Cheryl finally released her grip on Nina's arm and her voice was controlled when she said, "Well, you'll make an excellent witness for the prosecution, won't you?"

"Remember," Nina answered, "anything that Mindy told me is hearsay and inadmissible at trial. So don't take out a contract on me."

"I don't contract out anything." Cheryl seemed completely calm now.

"I see. How did you do it, by the way? I mean, get the poison and everything."

"The poison was easy. I used nicotine. You just crumble the tobacco from a pack of cigarettes into a glass of water. Then you strain it and let it evaporate until it's highly concentrated. A few drops on the patch is all you need. Nicotine is highly toxic and easily administered transdermally."

"How do you know all this?"

"I read it in some true-crime book."

"Then what did you do? Just switch patches and wait for Barry to use it?"

"Right. I figured it was only a matter of time until Jonathan brought the boat out here and took Barry sailing. I always thought Jonathan would make a good suspect."

"How come?"

"Because I knew that he was the one giving Barry the patches. And that he got them in Canada. Then I got lucky when Mindy dropped out of the house and you came in."

"Why was that?"

"Because I also knew that you would be interested in Jonathan. And that he was the kind of guy who would tell you everything. Enough to incriminate himself, even though he hadn't done anything."

"So you would have proceeded in the same way whether or not I took Mindy's place?"

"Absolutely. The patch was already in place."

"You know what I think is the most despicable part of all of this?" Nina couldn't help but raise her voice.

"What's that?"

"Jonathan."

"What about him?"

"How can you justify setting him up for Barry's murder?"

"I thought you might be a little bit upset about that."

"A little bit upset. C'mon. I mean, just because you decide

that Barry has to go down, how can you explain bringing Jonathan down with him?"

"I never actually accused him of anything."

"No, you just dragged me out here so that I could elicit damaging information from him. And while we're on the topic, I must say that I resent your manipulating me like a pawn in your chess game."

"Nina, if you don't want to be manipulated, you're going to have to do a better job of protecting yourself."

Oh, great. Even Cheryl, a demented murderer, felt justified in playing shrink to Nina's psyche. "Skip the advice," Nina said. "I don't think you're in any position to give any."

"Maybe not."

"By the way, what was the story with that woman Kim? The one that Barry was with at Sunmist?"

"I don't know. She was just someone Barry picked up. I hear the police gave the poor thing quite a grilling. It must have scared her badly. Might put her off socializing for a while."

Nina stared out over the horizon and thought about Cheryl. She had so many layers, it was hard to figure her out. There was the tough, hard exterior and the fragile, damaged subcutaneous tissue. But what was beneath that? Was there some secret center, some true inner soul, some essential nature as yet unrevealed to Nina? Maybe Cheryl was just what you saw—a mixture of hard and soft, of her Housing Court persona and the forlorn abandoned adolescent that she tried to leave behind.

Nina felt a surge of tenderness and pity. She had to remind herself that however many layers there were, there were also sociopathic hormones coursing through Cheryl's veins, pumped by the heart of a murderer. And it made Nina nervous to think that she could work side by side, day after day, with a colleague and not ever notice that anything was wrong. Well, Nina told herself, it was hard to spot the socio-paths in Housing Court. Somehow they fit right in.

She turned her attention back to the beach. It was really quite beautiful, even though a series of recent storms had eroded the dunes down to little sand piles. Fortunately, the last one had skipped the eastern end of Fire Island. The towns farther west had been badly hit.

"Ready to go back?" Nina asked.

"I guess," Cheryl said in a monotone.

They walked back along the beach silently. As they climbed the stairway up to the boardwalk, they turned for a last look at the ocean. "Well, this vacation didn't exactly turn out the way you thought it would, did it?" asked Cheryl.

"Not exactly. For one thing, I didn't really have to worry about getting sunburned."

"No, you hardly got to the beach at all. The weather's been so crummy," she said sorrowfully.

So that's what Cheryl regretted. The weather. There was no point in digging around Cheryl to find some remorse for what she did. On some level, she had convinced herself that she was a local heroine.

Neither of them said much as they walked back along the boardwalk. But as the house came into view, they noticed a familiar figure standing on the deck. It was Detective Ferrari.

"Look who's here," Cheryl said. "Big surprise."

Nina felt depleted. She had an urge to get away from the whole mess. "You know, I think I'll stop over at Jonathan's," she said. "I'll see you later."

"I'd say much later." Cheryl walked up the steps toward the police officer.

CHAPTER 36

Nina knocked and actually waited for someone to yell "come in" before she entered. It was overly formal for Davis Park, but Nina was in a cautious mood. "Is Jonathan around?" she asked the woman who was sitting in the living room.

"He's in the shower," she answered. "He'll be out in a little while. Why don't you sit down."

"Okay, thanks. I'm Nina, a friend of Jonathan's."

"Yes, I know." Of course she did.

She sat down on one end of the couch. There was a plaster nude of a reclining woman on the coffee table. This was probably the sculpture that Jonathan had referred to at the Sunmist party last week.

Nina took a closer look at the piece. It was very abstract, really just a suggestion of a woman's torso. But she could see beauty in the way the planes flowed together. Maybe she was having some kind of breakthrough. "Nice piece," she said.

"Oh, thank you."

"Is it your work?"

"Yes, it's part of a series I did last year, when my sister was in town for a month. I got her to pose for me."

"How nice." She took a closer look at the artist. She was about Nina's age and clearly not from the Bronx. She had pedicured feet and used a polish so subtle in color that you could hardly tell it was there. Very classy. It made her nails look like little sea shells. But instead of getting defensive, Nina found herself taking another look at the piece of sculpture. "It's quite beautiful," she said. "Have you cast it in bronze?" She wasn't sure exactly what that meant, but it sounded properly respectful.

"As a matter of fact, I have. I'm going to be in a group show on Mercer Street in the fall."

Nina monitored herself for signs of resentment. There were none. Her eyes didn't roll back even a quarter of an inch, her mouth remained relaxed, lips unpursed and unsmirked. Her breathing remained regular, long and even, not splintering into snappy little sniffs. She was definitely having a breakthrough of some sort.

"How nice for you," Nina said. She listened to herself saying it. She sounded genuine. Don't push it, she thought. This might be temporary. She could relapse any minute. She cast about for a subject to change to. "Have you been out here all week?" she asked.

But then Jonathan walked in, with wet curls plastered to his head. In place of his many items of cotton clothing, he wore just one—a short bathrobe that revealed a pair of long, lean legs and shapely patrician feet. Good, Nina thought. If we do ever make it to the maternity ward, maybe I'll break the Fischman dachshund curse that has plagued so many generations.

"Nina," he said. "You're back."

"Yes. It's been a long day."

"Tell me what happened."

"I don't know if this is for public broadcast. I mean, I'm sure it will be immediately recycled into the public domain. But initially, at least, I'd like to tell my story to just one person."

The woman smiled, but didn't look like she was going anywhere. "It's too cold to sit outside," Jonathan said. "We could go to my room. Or over to the boat."

"The boat. Perfect." A truly private place.

"Okay, I'll get dressed. It'll only take a minute."

It did only take a minute. He returned wearing a gray sweatsuit that looked so worn, it might have been from his high school track team. The crotch was stretched out, hanging halfway to his knees. Nina reached out and felt the material. It was as soft as a baby's favorite blanket. "I'll bet this has been through the wash a couple of times," she said.

"Yeah, I have to keep the pants up with a piece of rope." He slipped on a pair of deck shoes and they headed over to the boat. Once out of sight of the house, he slipped his arm into hers and leaned toward Nina. "Alone at last," he whispered into her ear. It made the hairs on her neck stand up straight. She smiled weakly, which was how she felt. Weak, at least in the knees.

They climbed down into the cabin and Jonathan pulled her onto the couch next to him. "Want something to drink?" he asked.

"Actually, is there anything to eat? I'm starving. All I've had since breakfast is a few ounces of raw fish stuck to a couple of grains of rice."

"Let's see, I don't think I have much."

"I suppose we can't very well order out, can we?"

"Not really. How about smoked mozzarella on a bagel? I'll melt it down in the microwave."

"Sounds great." Smoked mozzarella was one of her favorite substances. She only regretted having gone so many decades before encountering it.

Jonathan disappeared into the kitchen for a minute and Nina heard the beeps of a microwave oven being operated. She slid back into the couch and savored the feeling of being taken care of. Not in a global sense, of course. It wasn't as if she was marrying some rich man who was going to worry about all the bills and give her a generous allowance for life. All some guy was doing was melting some cheese on a bagel. But in Nina's scheme of things, it felt like a great luxury at the moment.

She looked around the cabin. It really was an incredibly beautiful room, done all in cherry wood that practically glowed. Again, she monitored herself for signs of resentment. But Nina felt remarkably calm. Or if not calm, then at least devoid of defensiveness. A double breakthrough. First sculpture, then sailboats. Maybe next week, she'd take a trip down to Palm Beach, hang around the polo fields and see how she did there.

Jonathan came back in with the food and a cobalt-blue bottle of some kind of Welsh water. The water might be going a bit far, she thought. She shouldn't push herself too far upscale in one day. She drank it anyway.

He resettled himself next to her on the couch. "So what happened? Did you talk to Mindy?" he asked.

"I did. I had lunch with her and then I came back and talked to Cheryl. And guess what?"

"What?"

"You didn't kill Barry."

"No shit, Sherlock."

"No shit."

"I told you so," he mock-whined.

She told him everything, all about Mindy and the price of

sushi and Cheryl and their walk on the beach and Ferrari's appearance on the front deck. "The amazing thing about Cheryl," Nina said, "is that she's totally remorseless. Like the sex offender out West that encouraged the state to execute him, because he guaranteed that he'd just go out and do it again."

"Well, try to stay on her good side."

"What do you think will happen to her?" Nina asked.

"I'm not sure that I really care. I get the distinct impression that she was trying to pin the whole thing on me."

"And I almost fell for it."

"But you didn't." He smoothed back her hair. "You valiantly sought out the truth. You're my hero."

"In that case, maybe you'd be willing to reimburse me for the twenty-seven dollars I spent on lunch today." She knew she wasn't helping the mood, but she was too nervous to handle this seduction scene with any dignity.

"Nina, now that all this intrigue is out of the way, can we talk about us?"

"Us. Jonathan, to tell you the truth, I'm a little nervous about us."

"Why?"

"I don't know if there can be an us. Do you think we'd make a good couple? I mean, we're so much alike. Shouldn't people balance each other out more? I mean, not have an exactly matched set of neuroses?"

He didn't answer, just sat there watching her. Which made her even more nervous. "On the other hand," she said, "I also feel like we have nothing in common. Our backgrounds are so different; you live on the East Side. I don't know if I can relate to it."

"Nina, cut the crap."

It was what she needed to hear. "All right, I will. But you've got to understand. Embarking on yet another new relationship at this stage is nerve-racking. With my long history and all."

"You think I don't feel the same way? That I don't feel like I've been through the Hundred Years' War? Relationships are like life—they can be a real pain in the ass. But when you consider the alternative . . ."

"I know," she said. "I'm not ready for retirement yet. And I don't really consider myself a risk-aversive person. But there's something about this that feels different. Like if we make a decision to go ahead, it'll be permanent. I don't know why I feel that way. I usually don't, but I do now."

"But isn't that good? Doesn't that show more potential than feeling you're embarking on a one-night stand?"

"I don't know." She thought about it. "Somehow it's easier to be able to think, 'Hell, I can always get out of this.' "

"You *can* always get out of this. I'm not going to stalk you, like the way Cheryl stalked Barry."

"Yeah, look at that relationship. See how complicated these things can get?"

"I'm not Barry and you're not Cheryl," he said. "For that matter, you're not Barry and I'm not Cheryl."

She laughed. Her wave of anxiety receded, as if it had been a physical symptom, like nausea or pain. At last she felt calm enough to recognize a surge of sexual desire flood over her. She lay back on the couch and beckoned to Jonathan. "Come over here," she whispered.

He leaned over her and put his hand on her breast as he kissed her. After the kiss, he kept it there, stroking her breasts while she just lay there silently with her eyes closed, letting her pleasure mount.

This guy had a lot to offer. He clearly could do more than just melt cheese on a bagel. When she could stand it no more, she pulled off her shirt and unhooked her bra and let him pick up where he left off.

She wondered idly, as he continued his skillful manipulations of her body, whether this was a one-time-only deal. Whether this was stuff he trotted out solely on a first-time basis. She began to worry about what would happen next time and the times after that.

But then his tongue got into the act and Nina decided she really didn't care. And she stopped thinking at all for the rest of the night.

CHAPTER 37

The next morning, Nina went back to her house to brush, floss, and shower. She left Jonathan in a good mood. She was in a pretty good mood herself. He had turned out to be more than just a sensitive and considerate lover, which always sounded too much like some kind of social worker. He was also enthusiastic and motivated, careful to leave his neuroses outside the bedroom.

The day was beautiful. The humidity had finally plunged down to almost nothing and the sky was completely blue. It was still early, just after nine, but the house was already abuzz. Judging by the number of used coffee filters in the sink, they were on their third pot. Everyone was in attendance and the conversation was so animated that Nina could hear their voices from the boardwalk. The only person whose absence was easily noted was Cheryl.

"There you are," said Barbara, when Nina walked in.

"We were getting worried. We thought that Cheryl might have thrown you into the ocean."

"No, I spent the night with Jonathan." Might as well tell them all now. They'd find out soon enough.

"Well, it's about time," Barbara said.

"I wanted to wait until things were resolved."

"Well, things are resolved all right."

"What happened? I noticed that Ferrari was here."

"Yeah, Nina," Ira said. "You missed all the action."

"It was horrible," Harriet said. "You're lucky you missed it."

"What happened?" Nina asked again.

Estelle answered. "Well, when you came back from the beach with Cheryl, Ferrari was here waiting for her. As you noticed."

"Right."

"At first I thought she might s-split, but she marched right up to him and s-said in this very Joan Crawford voice, 'May I help you?' "

"She's really something." Charlie shook his head with what looked like admiration.

Uh-oh, Nina thought. Was Charlie developing an ill-timed crush on Cheryl? Talk about unavailable women!

"And Ferrari just s-said, in this very quiet and controlled way, 'I think there are a few matters that we need to discuss.' And Cheryl s-said, 'Should I call my lawyer?' And then he gave her Miranda warnings and everything."

"Just like on television," Ira said.

"And how did Cheryl react?"

"Well, she called her lawyer," Barbara said.

"Who did she call?" Nina had often wondered who she would call if she ever got arrested. Most of the attorneys she knew avoided criminal law like the plague.

"I can't remember his name. But when she got through

to him, she put Ferrari on the phone. And they made arrangements for her arraignment, as if they were planning a business lunch. It was all very civilized. And then he took her away."

"Did they take the ferry back? Or did he have some special kind of police boat?"

"Who knows? It's not exactly like we all went down to see her off."

The phone rang and Harriet picked it up. "Nina, it's for you," she said, and then mouthed silently, "Some guy. But not Jonathan."

Nina jumped, but then remembered that Tom didn't have the number out there. "Hello?" she asked.

"Nina, it's Brian."

"Is everything all right?" She had visions of her beloved tenement reduced to a smoking ruin.

"Yeah. I checked your answering machine."

"And the Publishers Clearing House people are coming to see me next week?"

"Not quite. But Tom did call. He said Annie got sick and they had to cut their trip short. So he wants to know if you'd like to join him. He still has almost a week left on the canoe rental."

"It's a generous offer, but I think I'm going to be busy for the next couple of days."

"Oh, really?"

"Yeah, a friend and I are taking his boat out to Montauk."

"A friend? Anybody I know?" That was one of the best things about Brian—his impressive Y.Q. Nina appreciated a man with a high Yenta Quotient.

"Nope, nobody you know."

"Okay. Have fun. But you might be passing up the opportunity of a lifetime. Tom said the weather's been great up there."

"I'll take my chances," Nina said. "After all, why paddle when you can sail?"